THE CHRISTMAS BARGAIN

THE CHRISTMAS BARGAIN

•

Sarita Leone

AVALON BOOKS
NEW YORK

ʳ
Le o

Published by Avalon Books, an imprint of
Thomas Bouregy & Co., Inc.
160 Madison Avenue, New York, NY 10016

Library of Congress Cataloging-in-Publication Data

Leone, Sarita.
    The Christmas bargain / Sarita Leone.
        p. cm.
    ISBN 978-0-8034-7797-1 (hardcover : acid-free paper)
    1. Young women—England—Fiction.   2. Mate selection—
Fiction.   3. Aristocracy (Social class)—England—Fiction.
4. Christmas stories.   I. Title.
    PS3612.E578C47 2010
    813'.6—dc22

                                                      2010018148

PRINTED IN THE UNITED STATES OF AMERICA
ON ACID-FREE PAPER
BY HADDON CRAFTSMEN, BLOOMSBURG, PENNSYLVANIA

For Vito Leone, the man who brings love, laughter, and sunshine to my world. You are my hero, my strong, brave man. My inspiration, I will love you forever.

Chapter One

Iris Newgate paced the chilly, damp drawing room like a caged animal.

She strode from window to window, pulling back the heavy velvet drapes and looking out at the gray, dreary world. Every time she peeked, the same view met her gaze: a cobblestone street grimy and splattered with soggy brown lumps left by scores of work-weary horses drawing carriages. Rain falling incessantly, hard enough to add to the already bone-shaking feel of the day.

Despite her stubborn refusal to believe that which became clearer with each passing moment, there was no sign of the one thing she looked for, hoped for—a proper prospective suitor to save her from a fate worse than death. There was no sign of the earl's carriage. None whatsoever, no matter how diligently she scanned the street for a glimpse of the man's lavish conveyance.

There was no help for it. Her heart fell a little lower into the pit of her stomach with each *tick-tock-tick* of the mantel clock. She cast a worried glance at the timepiece for what felt like

1

the hundredth time in the past hour. *A quarter past.* It would not have been so terribly awful if the fifteen minutes were just beyond the appointed meeting hour. But *two hours* and a quarter? That was too much for even a woman of her forgiving nature to overlook.

Iris sighed, dragging air from so deep within her body that her toes curled inside the too-tight yet fashionable side-button shoes she wore. She plopped down onto the nearest settee and lifted her gaze three feet higher than the clock. Grandfather's steely gray eyes, so menacing in the portrait, stared down at her. He had been gone for two Seasons, yet Iris could hear him as clearly as if he stood in the room beside her.

His gravelly voice—feared by business associates for its cut-to-the-chase honesty but adored by his only granddaughter because for her it held love—filled her head now.

Such a bounder will get his comeuppance in the afterlife. You need to focus on doing what is best for you here and now. Stand up, child, and face the future. It's the only way to show you don't have more hair than wit, my dear.

Dutifully Iris stood. Her legs were wobbly, but she forced her spine to straighten. Grandfather was right. If she was to find a suitable man to marry—and the Earl of Hampfordshire was undeniably *un*suitable!—she had to concentrate on moving forward. She had to have a plan, one that would insure her happiness in the future.

After all, she was a Newgate. She had to be strong. Sure of herself. Determined. Sharing a name with London's main prison, the place where so many met with the executioner's hand, had to count for something, didn't it? Surely it did, even if Iris herself thought justice was best left to a higher power than the hangman's knot.

Yes, she would formulate a plan. One that did not include

the errant earl. Then she would carry it out. By Christmas, she would be betrothed. She had to be. If she wasn't, she would be forced to wed the most despicable, detestable, and utterly reprehensible scoundrel she had the sad misfortune to be acquainted with. Well, *almost* acquainted with.

Before Iris allowed the reading of the banns announcing her impending nuptials to Lord James Whitman, she would throw herself at Grandfather's barrister's feet and beg for mercy—or marriage. Edgar Clark had to be eighty if he was a day, but he was still greatly preferable to Lord Whitman, the Duke of Willingham. At least Mr. Clark had never killed a man. And, if the whispers of polite society were to be believed, the mysterious Lord James Whitman had likely murdered several men. In cold blood, apparently.

No, Iris would never consent to marry a fake and murderer. Never. There had to be some other way. . . .

Two weeks later, the drawing room was neither chilly nor damp. Nor was it the same dreary, oppressive space it had been when Iris waited with futile anticipation for a new suitor's arrival.

Laughter and gaiety, as well as a crackling fire, made the drawing room an altogether different space entirely. Iris and her closest friends, embroidery hoops in hands, chatted the afternoon away with no mind—or very little—to the past. They concentrated on the future. Iris' future, to be precise.

Catherine, her blond hair touched by highlights from the glow of the fire, tied off a French knot before looking up from her work. The daughter of one of the wealthiest men in the city, she was as beautiful as her father was rich. Her betrothal had been in place for ages.

The man intended for Catherine's match, Ethan Daniel

Harding, the Earl of Gloucester, currently journeyed abroad. When he returned, their plans would continue posthaste. Catherine was eager to marry and start a family. Iris' difficulty securing a suitable husband was almost more than Catherine's delicate nature could withstand.

"I still can't believe your grandfather put that codicil into his will." Catherine shook her head, sending a curl tumbling over her forehead. She pushed it back with one palm while she dug in her sewing basket with the other hand. "Imagine, setting your future up with that dastardly Lord Whitman! Why, the rogue is known far and wide as one of the most disreputable men to walk among polite society! How could your grandfather be so cruel?"

"I don't believe Grandfather thought he was being cruel," Iris insisted. She had had plenty of time to consider the matter, and if there was one thing she was certain of, it was that Mr. Clark and Grandfather had brought about this situation with her paramount interest at heart. Grandfather would never do anything to make her unhappy. She was positive of the fact. "I think he did what he thought was best." That was, she knew in her heart, the complete truth.

"You're saying he didn't know the man's nefarious nature?" Catherine looked wide-eyed at the possibility. Her lower lip quivered, a hand shielded her heart, and she held her breath.

" 'Nefarious,' my foot!" The eldest at three and twenty, Lady Bridget Miles, recently married and therefore the ultimate voice of experience, waved a hand in the air between them. Her dark eyes flashed scorn, and her brow, so clear and unblemished, pulled together into a tight frown. "I think all that talk about Lord Whitman is rubbish. Nothing more than the *ton* having more time than purpose on its hands."

Iris looked over the edge of the sampler she was working on. Its intricate, curlicued lettering gave her a headache. Her eyes, grateful for the respite, blinked rapidly at Bridget's statements.

Everyone who was anyone had heard the gossip about Lord Whitman. It had gone on for years, changing slightly each Season and growing more outlandish with every passing year. It was, essentially, the story of a rogue without any principles. A man whose gambling, womanizing, and general disregard for anything God-fearing, genteel, or conscionably appropriate painted a truly despicable picture.

When she had learned the stipulation of Grandfather's will, that she either marry a man of her own choosing or become betrothed to Lord Whitman within the span of four and twenty months, Iris initially felt as if her life was at an end. It was as if she had succumbed to the same heart-stopping ailment that had claimed the man who had taken her in when she was an infant and her parents were killed in a carriage accident. Iris was devastated by the news from the legal document and welcomed the death she knew must surely be close at hand.

But death, as with so many other things in life, surprised her. It did not come for her but, rather, left her to fend for herself. Left her to snare a suitable match during the Season or, failing that, to marry Lord Whitman as per Grandfather's codicil. The penalty for doing neither left her with a trifling bank account and an abandoned, tumbledown cottage. Ignoring Grandfather's bequest painted a dismal future for Iris, one that she hoped to avoid.

"What makes you say that? That the gossip is untrue?" Iris asked quietly. Hope lifted her heart at the same instant reality pushed it back into place. There was no likelihood that Bridget spoke anything other than what she wanted to believe, or what she wanted to convince Iris was fact. No likelihood at all. There couldn't be.

Without looking up from her sewing, Bridget shrugged. She deftly licked the end of the length of canary yellow floss in her hand before threading it through the eye of her needle. She plunged the needle into her linen and began to stitch.

"Oh, I don't know," Bridget finally said. She kept her gaze averted as she went on, her tone deceptively nonchalant. "I just don't believe your grandfather would attach you—in any way at all—to a scoundrel. There's got to be more to Lord Whitman's story, something we don't yet know." Scowling as a red spot showed on the tip of one finger, Bridget dropped her work into her lap and stuck her fingertip between her lips. She sucked thoughtfully for a long, silent moment. Then, pulling her finger from her mouth with a wet, popping sound, she smiled. "Your grandfather loved you far too much to match you up with a horrid man. There must be something redeeming about Lord Whitman. Something your grandfather knew but wanted you to discover for yourself."

Catherine put aside her sewing. She sat back and lifted each shoulder in turn, rotating the stiffness from them. They had been engaged with their samplers for well over an hour, and the work, although satisfying, was tedious.

"Any chance this is a setup by dear old Grandfather?" Catherine teased. A shadow passed before her eyes. She, and Bridget as well, had loved the old man. They had both referred to him as Grandfather in private since they wore short skirts. "You know the kind. A mystery of sorts for you to figure out? Kind of a giggle from the grave?"

Iris contemplated the possibility. Grandfather *had* enjoyed teasing her. Perhaps this situation, which had her at sixes and sevens, wasn't such a bumblebroth after all. Perhaps it was all part of a bigger plan, a good plan laid out through Grandfather's careful consideration. Perhaps—

The drawing room door opened wide. Ethel Fenwick, the housekeeper, stood in the doorway in her starched uniform. Her expression was one of complete puzzlement.

"Yes, Ethel?" Iris pulled her lips into a polite smile. "What can I do for you?"

"There's a gentleman at the door, miss." Ethel hesitated. She cleared her throat before she went on. "He says he wants to see you. Naturally I said he hadn't made an appointment, that you weren't expecting him, and that you were already entertaining visitors, but . . ."

"But what?"

Ethel swallowed. "But he insists, miss. He says he will only take a few moments of your time. He says you . . . he says you'll want to see him when I announce him."

Iris looked at her companions. Their expressions were equal to the one on the maid's face. Pushing aside exasperation, Iris took a deep breath. What else could life possibly throw her way?

"For goodness' sake, Ethel." Iris purposefully kept her voice calm even though her innards had begun to flutter. "Who is it?"

"It's . . . ah . . . it's Lord Whitman, miss."

Chapter Two

Dear heaven, what on earth can *he* want?" Catherine's embroidery slid off her lap. It pooled unnoticed at her feet, completely covering the tips of her blue velvet slippers. Her hand, so small and white, went to her throat, and, had Iris not been so shocked, she might have laughed at her friend's apparent distress. Anyone would have thought the man in question had come to see Catherine instead of Iris!

She turned back to the housekeeper, who still stood stock-still in the open doorway. She raised one eyebrow in silent question; Ethel gave a clipped nod, so sharp it caused the edge of her white day cap to slide forward a bit. It gave the work-weary, middle-aged widow a slightly come-hither look. Iris pressed her lips together, determined not to smile despite the silly appearance the tilted cap gave the servant.

It seemed the only one not descending into comedic stupor was Bridget. Perhaps it was her age that gave her the where-withal to withstand the arcane. Perhaps they could all take a lesson from Bridget, one in decorum under duress. Perhaps—

Then again, maybe not. When Iris swiveled her head to her

right, where Bridget sat on the chair beside he.
ture of Bridget as she had never seen her befo.
doubted anyone had ever seen the unflappable L.
Miles looking so . . . well, *flapped.*

Bridget's mouth hung agape. Had it been June instea
tober, there would have been, undoubtedly, flies buzzing ... ound
her molars. As it was, Bridget's open mouth was blessedly insect free, but it was also, Iris realized with a start, breathless.

She poked Bridget in the arm, sending her friend's body
tipping sideways a few inches.

"Breathe, Bridget! You're going to fall over onto your face
if you don't start inhaling again," Iris urged, poking her a second time. This time Bridget pulled her mouth shut, her teeth
clicking together with what could only have been a somewhat
uncomfortable snap. "That's better. At least you don't look like
a goldfish now. But do be careful. I don't want to be responsible for your breaking your teeth."

"I'm not going to break anything," Bridget huffed. She inhaled, then exhaled in a long, shuddering *whoosh* that puffed
her cheeks out, making her look still more fishlike.

Catherine covered her mouth and tittered, which made Iris
giggle.

"Yes, she does look like one of the goldfish in Father's
pond, now that you mention it." Catherine nodded emphati-
cally, her own shock forgotten at Bridget's expense. "Very
fishlike, actually."

"Pish, posh!" Bridget swatted at the giggling pair with her
embroidery hoop. The yellow floss she had so carefully
threaded fluttered through the air like the tail of a kite. "A goldfish! Really, now—how ridiculous!"

"Well, if the shoe fits . . ." Iris agreed.

"That's right," laughed Catherine. She ran a fingertip beneath her right eye and wiped away the tear pooling beneath it. "The shoe and the fish. If they fit—"

A decidedly male voice cut Catherine off short. It filled the room, bringing an abrupt end to the trio's laughter. Their giggles died in their throats. They sat as still as if they had each been turned into a pillar of salt. One small gasp, from Catherine, was the only sound save the man's observation.

"Fish? Shoes?" He paused theatrically. "How in the world can one put shoes on a fish? Where does one fit the fins?"

Lord James Whitman stood tall, his figure so muscular and wide that Ethel was practically dwarfed by comparison. He filled the doorway, his shoulders nearly touching both sides of the doorjamb. His morning coat, with its wide lapels and padded shoulders, exaggerated his already well-cut physique.

Iris stared at him for a long moment without replying. She had never before been this close to the man and had not realized how very attractive he actually was. Whenever she had seen him previously, it had been at a distance—through a window or across a crowded ballroom—so this up-close display stunned her.

How could one man cut such a debonair figure yet still be such a ne'er-do-well? It defied comprehension.

Bridget's elbow, nudging her not so gently in her side, brought Iris out of her musing. She remembered her manners and, hoping Lord Whitman would not notice her open appraisal, smiled.

"It was, I assure you, merely idle conversation," Iris said, widening her smile. She remained seated but inclined her head slightly. "We had no idea anyone was listening to our prattle, Lord Whitman."

"Ah, I see." His thick black curls showed signs of having been rained on recently, but instead of looking disheveled, the man seemed perfectly at home standing with droplets dripping onto his shoulders. He smiled, and it was as if a breeze had blown through the room, dimming the lamps and casting everything—and everyone—else into shadow. Two rows of glistening white teeth hypnotized Iris for a moment. When she realized that his eyes—a deep navy blue rimmed around the irises with a black ring—sparkled, she gave herself a mental shake. She opened her mouth to speak but was cut off by his next words. "So, you did not expect me, then?"

Iris shook her head. "No." She swallowed, searching for a polite way to go on. Her mind was almost as empty as the leafless trees outside in Grandfather's garden. "We did not know you were coming. Was your servant meant to drop a calling card yesterday? Or the day before, perhaps? Perhaps it was meant to be left but was an oversight?"

With a chuckle, he stepped into the room more fully. Two steps and his long legs brought him substantially nearer. "No, it wasn't an oversight, although I appreciate your allowing me a way out of my social bumble. But, alas, I cannot fib. I did not dispatch any of my servants with a calling card. I did not want to afford you the opportunity to refuse my visit, Miss Newgate."

A shiver of trepidation shot up Iris' spine. She sat straighter, as if a post on the chair behind her had threaded itself up the back of her frock.

Honest. At least, in this instance, the man was honest. He had not sent a card, had not wanted to be refused, and had been man enough to admit as much. The admission surprised her, but there was no time to dwell on it. Lord Whitman spoke again.

"So, you see, I am afraid I am unannounced. Unexpected. And perhaps unwanted." He took two more steps closer and leaned over the back of the wing chair directly across from where Iris sat. She smiled at his forthrightness, but her smile had barely creased her face when it vanished. Catherine, full in a tizzy, responded rudely.

"I should say so!" she gasped. She fluttered a hand before her cheeks. They had bright splotches of pink on them. "Intrusive at the very least."

Whitman's eyebrows shot up at Catherine's words. He looked at her; beneath his scrutiny Catherine's cheeks colored deeper, and she closed her mouth like a clam out of water. The man turned slowly, bringing his gaze to meet Iris'. One eyebrow went higher, questioningly.

Iris swallowed. How to salvage the moment? *Grace under pressure.* Grandfather had always said she kept her head when others lost theirs. She prayed he was right. Her hands shook, but she threaded her fingers together and laid them on her lap.

"So to what do we owe the pleasure of your visit, Lord Whitman?" Iris nodded her chin toward the chair across from her, noticing for the first time that he held a riding crop loosely in one hand. It dangled over the chair back, nearly touching the brocade seat. "Please, have a seat. May I have Mrs. Fenwick get you some tea?"

Bridget's shocked gasp was the only sound in the room for a split second. It seemed loud, but fortunately the visitor did not notice. Or if he did, he again overlooked the rudeness.

Lord Whitman stood up straight, slapping one palm with the folded crop. The noise made Iris cringe—inwardly, for she refused to flinch before anyone—but she held his gaze steadily. Finally he shook his head, sending one thick, black lock falling across his brow. He left it there, which made it supremely difficult for Iris to keep herself from staring at his lush, curly cap. It fairly begged to be touched. Mussed. Fondled.

Swallowing hard, Iris again fixed her stare on Lord Whitman's eyes. They looked amused. Very amused. He couldn't know what she thought, could he? Who could tell with a rogue?

"No, thank you," he finally said. The words brought relief—and disappointment. "I did not come to partake of tea, although that is a very fine offer—one I hope to indulge with you in the future." Lord Whitman glanced at Catherine and Bridget and then turned his attention back to Iris. "In the very *near* future, with *you,* Miss Newgate," he added. There was no room to misinterpret his words. But there was not time to examine them, either. Lord Whitman continued.

"I came with the hope of determining whether or not you will be in attendance at the Fall Fete at—"

"At Lady Hargrove-Smythe's," Bridget briskly interrupted, leaving the man to snap his mouth closed with a startled, annoyed look. She shrugged, as if speaking to a mental patient, and said slowly, "Of course Iris knows where the Fall Fete is to be held, Lord Whitman. Everyone knows of it. Absolutely everyone!"

He scowled at Bridget. Iris noted that even when he was perturbed, he was exceedingly handsome—in a rakish sort of manner, of course. "Right. Duly noted, Miss—uh, Lady Miles." The slight was obvious, but he continued smoothly, turning his attention back to Iris. "It is the final London party for this year, and everyone who remains in Town will be in attendance. I simply wondered if you, Miss Newgate, would also be at the affair."

Iris' mouth felt as dry as the Sahara desert at high noon. With an eye toward buying a few seconds with which to contemplate a reply, she nervously licked her lips. The room was silent, with everyone waiting for her to speak. There was no way to get out of answering, and even if she had been inclined to lie—which she most certainly was not—there was no need.

Everyone would see whether or not she attended the Fall Fete.
What harm could there be in answering the man's question?

Nodding, Iris said, "Yes. I will be at Lady Hargrove-
Smythe's Fall Fete."

A smug grin fixed itself firmly on Lord Whitman's face. He
nodded, then turned and walked to the door. Passing the housekeeper, he called over his shoulder, "I pray you will save at least
one—possibly all—of the waltzes for me, Miss Newgate. Good
day, now!"

They heard the front door close. Then his horse's hoofbeats
faded into the distance.

Years had passed since James had last seen Iris Newgate,
and he had not been prepared to find her so lovely. Her creamy
porcelain complexion, high cheekbones, and luminous emerald green eyes caught him off guard. He had known her to be
a fetching young thing, but the woman she had become was
startlingly beautiful. Even more startling was the fact that it
was obvious, just from the few moments they had spent together, that Iris had no idea she was simply stunning.

Her mouth, naturally colored a shade of rose usually reserved
for garden flowers, was the shape of a bow, and, like the finish-
ing touch to a precious parcel, it completed her. Her lips called
to him as sweetly as nectar calls a honeybee, and it had taken
every ounce of self-restraint he possessed not to stride across
the room and taste those tender lips for himself.

But it wasn't only Iris Newgate's appearance that stuck with
him. Even now, nearly halfway to his own London town house,
James could not get over the impression she had given that
she was not at all an average woman, intelligence-wise. Every
one of her actions, comments, and expressions showed with-

out reserve that within the outer trappings of beauty she possessed a keen mind and sharp wit.

Her mind, mayhap even more than her body, brought James' interest to full alert. Pretty faces came at a price; a woman with superior intelligence could be priceless to the right man. A man like himself.

Chapter Three

"Must you play such a dreary selection? Honestly, I feel as if I am part of a funeral procession rather than a . . . well, pre-party." Bridget turned, casting a shrewd stare at Catherine, who sat pounding out the offensive notes on the finely tuned parlor instrument. "Come, come! Let us hear something gay and pretty for a change. Enough of that somber tone. It really does sound like a funeral march!"

Catherine brought her fingers down hard on the keys. The pianoforte, a gift to Iris from her grandfather on her tenth birthday, groaned. With a swirl of her skirts, Catherine stood and swept across the room. She stopped beside Bridget and Iris, looked down at the lengths of ribbon and lace strewn about them on the deep burgundy velvet sofa, and snorted. The very unladylike noise brought the others to instant attention.

"It may as well be a funeral march I play," Catherine said. She stamped her foot once, but it was a small, useless action designed, as they well knew, more for effect than anything else. "I can't believe the two of you—going on about gowns and bonnets and lace and gloves! And whatever for? To impress that detestable man? To cover Iris' fingers in fine lace in order that she hold the hand of the devil himself while she waltzes? It's—it's—it's absurd, that's what it is. And shame on you, Bridget, for encouraging her in this—this—" She opened and closed her mouth several times before she finished. "This charade!"

"I'm not encouraging her. And it is not a charade, you silly goose. We're preparing for a real, live social opportunity, one where our Iris may meet a suitable man. Let's not lose sight of the fact that you-know-who won't be the only eligible bachelor in attendance." Bridget wrapped a length of red ribbon around her fingertips, winding it tightly enough to stuff it back into the notions box. She had already stated she thought red an unsuitable color for Iris' complexion. "Iris may find someone, even at this late date, to satisfy the terms of Grandfather's will. One never knows. . . ."

Iris would have loved nothing more than to ignore them. Both had already made their positions clear, but clarity and opinion were not solutions to her problem. No, she needed to do whatever she must in order to wiggle her way out of an enforced marriage to a man who, as her friends so aptly put it, made Satan look like a choirboy. Heaven help her, but she was not going to fall willingly into the rogue's arms. Not if she could help it. If that meant she must dress up and smile at every last marriageable man in London, that's exactly what she was going to do.

Releasing the sigh she had been holding, Iris reached for Catherine's hand. She pulled her down onto the sofa beside her, not paying any mind to the satins and lace she crushed. Then she took one of Bridget's hands in her free hand and, thus joined with her friends, took a deep, steadying breath.

She looked up and glanced quickly from woman to woman before she spoke.

"You are my closest friends," she said quietly. She squeezed the hands she held, drawing warmth and strength from both. "With Grandfather gone, I have no one . . . that is, no one except the two of you. Someday, God willing, I will have a husband and a family to call my own, but for now, I've got the two of you. And I am heartily grateful for that." A lump formed in Iris' throat, and she swallowed hard to push it down. It abated but only slightly. With more determination than before, she pressed on. "We know what I must do. A woman doesn't have many choices in this world; I must follow the path Grandfather laid out before me. He loved me, and I know he watches me from heaven. I know he had a reason for putting me smack-dab into this situation. If my heart is open and my faith does not falter, I believe I will see my way clear of this mess. Now, please, help me do what I know I must. I need your help. Bridget." Iris met their gazes one after the other. "Catherine. Please." The last word was a near whisper.

Two hands squeezed Iris', gently but firmly. Bridget reached out and clasped Catherine's free hand, closing the circle. Wordlessly they bowed their heads.

"Heavenly Father, we come to you in supplication and faith." Bridget's voice was strong, and it lifted Iris. "You know Iris' predicament. We know you have a plan for her, please show us your path so we may help her take the first steps toward whatever it is you have in store for her. Amen."

"Amen," Iris whispered. Renewed hope filled her, pushing aside some—but not all—of the fear that had been plaguing her since Lord Whitman's unorthodox intrusion.

"Amen," Catherine echoed. With a smile, she dropped their hands and clapped hers together like a schoolmarm calling a class to order. "So! What's next? Trimming gloves or choosing a color for your gown? And when, pray tell, do we head to the dressmaker's? Time is running short, ladies—or had you forgotten?"

Astonishment crossed Bridget's face, pulling her features into a parody of sublime shock.

As Catherine stood, her full skirts swishing around her ankles, and flounced back to the pianoforte, Iris laughed. Leave it to these two to pull sunshine from a storm cloud!

"I'm not sure if that exact shade of green is your color," Bridget said thoughtfully. She looked up at Mrs. Martin, the proprietress of L. Martin's Fine Dresses, and asked, "Do you have it in anything deeper? A forest green, perhaps? Something to bring out her eyes, make her look more vibrant?"

The middle-aged widow, accustomed to requests of this nature, cocked her head and crossed her arms over her ample bosom. She wore a serviceable brown work dress that didn't advertise her sewing abilities well, but, with her reputation, the brown dress was all that was needed. The beautiful gowns Mrs. Martin created were enticement enough for every lady in London to seek out her services. Had it been during the Season, Iris, Bridget, and Catherine never would have waited so long to peruse her fabrics. But with the last affair before the holidays on the docket, and so many women wearing leftover gowns to the Fete, waiting until the late date was not imprudent.

Tapping her chin lightly with the tip of her index finger, Mrs. Martin said, "That color isn't exactly right, is it? Makes her look sort of washed out, don't you think?"

"Exactly what I thought!" Bridget nodded in agreement. It was a good thing the laces beneath her chin were firmly tied. Had they not been, her velvet bonnet would have toppled off her head and onto the floor. "Washed out. Sallow, almost, don't you think?"

"*Sallow*—that's the word I had in mind," Catherine agreed.

Catherine sat on one side of Iris; Bridget sat on the other. Between them Iris felt like a flower beneath a botanist's probing eye. A droopy, washed-out flower at that.

"Yes, definitely sallow." With a *humph* and a wave of one chubby hand, Mrs. Martin hurried from the room. They heard her in the next room, rummaging through the racks of fine fabrics she kept for her "best" customers. The trio looked at one another with suppressed grins. Everyone knew that each and every woman who passed beneath the hand-painted sign above the door into L. Martin's Fine Dresses was a "best" customer.

A pile of discards lay draped across a blue velvet chaise. The gowns were already made and would need only a nip here and a tuck there, a bit of discreet alteration to make them suitable to all but the stoutest figure. For any of them to suit Iris' slender frame, the dressmaker's task would have been undemanding—at most a day's work. Unfortunately none of the ready-made gowns satisfied the trio. They each brought a keen eye and a distinct taste in fashion to the outing. Finding something that suited everyone was never straightforward but was generally accomplished with a minimum amount of fuss. But this gown had to be spectacular, and, as such, its procurement was going to be less trouble-free than that of more everyday garments.

Catherine rose and walked across the room to the chaise longue. She leaned down and pushed a violet silk gown aside with one long fingernail. It was amazing that she kept her nails intact, given the hours she spent playing the pianoforte. But so many things about Catherine were spectacular and had always been so. Her fair beauty and scatterbrained view of the world—they had been engaging when Iris, Bridget, and Catherine were younger but were even more so now. It was no wonder Catherine had caught the eye of her well-heeled, dashing betrothed.

"It is too bad indeed that this does not suit you better." She held up a filmy, bias-cut, formfitting gown in a sultry shade of red. "With your coloring this should work, but this skirt, with its overlay, brings the whole profile down. Don't you agree, Bridget?"

A sideways glance and a twitch of her lips told the full extent of Bridget's opinion. Iris had to agree; the color was fabulous, but the skirt looked designed with dowdiness—as well as the mission to conceal a flabby stomach—in mind.

"That one? It is dreadful," Bridget pronounced. Her open disapproval and the confidence that swept off her in waves once again reinforced the distinction that she was a married woman, while Iris and Catherine were not. There was just a tilt to the head of a married woman, a sureness that came with the placement of a wedding band on a manicured finger, that Bridget possessed. It set the women slightly apart. It was an acknowledged fact of their lives, one that neither Catherine nor Iris begrudged their dearest friend. They both knew that eventually they would also have a married woman's confidence, as well as that certain extra tilt to their chins.

"Let's hope there is magic behind those curtains," Catherine said, nodding in the direction the shopkeeper had taken. "Magic and mystery, glamour and sparkle, and all for Iris! Oh, yes, I do believe that is exactly what we need to have Iris make a splash at the Fall Fete!" She clapped her hands together. The gesture was charming coming from Catherine, and the other two smiled broadly at her optimism.

Personally, Iris was less optimistic. But she was smart enough to keep her thoughts to herself, especially since the others were so positive that she would succeed.

When she emerged from the storage room, Mrs. Martin carried a gown in emerald green velvet that was so striking, all three women gasped in unison.

"Ooh!" breathed Catherine, fluttering a hand before her face.

"Now, that's more what I had in mind," said Bridget. She took an edge of fabric between her fingertips and rubbed. "Much better, both in color and quality."

Mrs. Martin nodded, her jowls bouncing as she hurried to say, "Well, of course I keep only the finest for my best customers. And Miss Newgate . . . well, she's one of my *very* best."

All attention turned to Iris. She felt their scrutiny and was, for a moment, overwhelmed.

The dress was beautiful, far plusher than any gown she owned. The color was like none she had seen before. She wondered why Mrs. Martin hadn't made any other gowns with the stunning shade during the Season but did not ask. It did not matter anyway, did it?

In that instant Iris grappled with a small inner crisis. She looked up from the gown to the gazes so intent on her, then back down to the pool of emerald velvet spread across her lap. Her heartbeat stuttered, falling prey to the doubt that plagued her. What if a gorgeous gown—even one of such a wondrous hue—wasn't enough to capture the attention of a proper would-be husband at the Fall Fete?

And, although she had pronounced any man more suitable than the one Grandfather had foisted upon her, Iris knew the truth. She couldn't marry just *any* man. She *wouldn't* marry simply any man. Not for any reason, regardless of what Grandfather wanted or her protestations led anyone to believe.

The man she would marry had to capture her heart. And she

his. A fairly tall order, even for a dress sewn of magnificent, jewel-toned fabric.

Releasing a long, shuddering sigh, Iris lifted her gaze to meet the dressmaker's. "This will do perfectly," she said, sounding much more self-assured than she felt.

Chapter Four

Fall's frosty fingers found their way beneath the heavy lap blanket that covered Iris from the waist down. She shivered and then tried to bring summer's sultry breezes to mind, hoping the illusion would warm her more fully than the carriage blanket did. Mayhap if she conjured the scent of roses to inhale rather than the moldy leaf odor kicked up by the horses' hooves, or brought to mind the sound of gay chatter to cover the dismal silence of the late-day gloom, she might feel some semblance of merriment. Or if she pulled the . . .

It was no use. Neither conjuring nor wishing could change the bare facts of the afternoon. She was out of sorts. It was cold, and the nippiness that stung her cheeks only served to make her foul mood fouler.

Perhaps a ride in the park had not been the best idea after all. It had seemed a sensible—nay, an adventurous—thing to do only an hour earlier. The walls of Grandfather's library had felt as if they were closing in on her, and the freedom afforded by a carriage ride had seemed the ideal antidote to soothe her frayed nerves. But the day had not cooperated, weather-wise, and what was to have been fun now felt frustrating.

Still, it would hardly do to waste an hour out-of-doors. And as the lumbering carriage rounded a corner, one of Iris' favorite spots in the entire park came into view. Some of her foul temper fled, and a smile twitched the edges of her lips upward.

A grove of poplar trees, their thin, silvery trunks blending into the streaky gray sky, dominated this secluded corner of the park. During the summer, the coin-shaped, light green leaves on the poplars rustled together so smoothly, the trees sounded as if they were whispering. Many afternoons she and Grandfather had picnicked beneath these very trees, their luncheon punctuated by giggles, laughter, and speculation about what sort of dialogue poplar trees could actually have.

Oh, Grandfather had indulged her in so many ways, nurturing her heart and soul more fully than her own two parents might have. Truthfully, Iris had never missed her parents, never lamented her situation, never yearned to have anything—or anyone—other than what fate had bestowed upon her.

Until now, that is. Now she missed Grandfather. His subtle guidance, his loving words, his sage advice . . . all was lost to her, and now, for the first time in her life, she felt alone.

Without regard for the coolness of the day, she leaned forward and opened the conversation window between the compartment and the driver's seat. "Stop the carriage, please." Before Jackson could reply, Iris snapped the window closed. She knew what the elderly driver's reaction would be before she spoke. Better not to give him the chance to voice his protests.

For a long moment she wondered if Jackson was going to pretend not to have heard her request. The horses continued forward, pulling completely abreast of the poplars, before she saw his arms draw back on the reins and felt the carriage wheels slow.

Iris did not wait for Jackson to open her door. She threw the lap blanket aside, reached toward the door, and turned the latch. The door sprang open, letting an icy gust of air sweep into the carriage's interior, but Iris refused to be deterred. Gathering her long skirts around her legs, she stepped out of her conveyance and onto the dead brown grass at the lane's edge.

"It's more than a mite chilly out here, Miss Newgate." Jackson turned up the collar on his driving coat and shivered dramatically. His movement was exaggerated enough that he could have been in a stage performance. "You don't want to catch your death in the park, do you?"

"Certainly not. I'd rather not 'catch' my death anywhere, Jackson." Iris let a small grin dart across her face. The notion of hunting down, then capturing, one's own death was amusing. "And I'm more than adequately dressed for the weather." Since Jackson was also warmly attired, Iris felt no guilt when she told him her plan. "I'm going to take a short stroll beneath the trees over there. You know the ones I mean. I know you do; you brought Grandfather and me here more times than I can remember."

"Quite true, miss. But if I recall correctly, your grandfather favored warmer days than this for your outings." The driver's bushy white eyebrows knit. He shot a meaningful glance at the gray clouds scudding across the steely sky.

Iris chose to ignore his pointed expression. She took two steps away from the carriage, the heels of her sensible traveling boots moving easily over the near-frozen ground.

Jackson and Mrs. Fenwick, as well as the head cook, Mrs. Perkins, and Emma Jean, Iris's lady's maid, had all taken it upon themselves to fill in for Grandfather after his passing.

Each in his or her own small way had tried to advise, amuse, or coddle Iris to some extent. She had allowed it—to a degree—because she recognized their love and affection, as well as the honorable intentions, behind their words and deeds.

Now, however, was not the time to indulge Jackson's desire that she remain cocooned in the spacious carriage. Keeping her gaze firmly on the poplar grove, Iris replied, "Grandfather isn't here to approve or disapprove of my choice of days. I shan't be long, Jackson. Just a short stroll."

Striding off toward the trees brought the burst of freedom Iris had hoped it would. The long ends of her bonnet ribbons pressed against her chest as a gust of wind hit her hard. It lasted but a moment, and when it dissipated, she straightened her shoulders and pressed forward. She knew where she was going, the destination as plain in her mind as if it had been in view. A minute or two of brisk walking would bring her to the spot.

Iris ducked beneath one especially low-hanging branch, taking care not to snag her bonnet on the long, brittle twigs that stuck out at odd angles. The last time she had been here with Grandfather, she had caught her headgear on the very same branch and torn one ribbon completely off the frippery on its right side. A periwinkle blue ribbon, it had been. When she had reached for it, Grandfather's hand took hers and pulled it to his lips. He had given her a kiss, his bristly mustache tickling her skin despite her gloves, and a suggestion that they leave the dangling ribbon for a swallow or chickadee to use to feather a nest.

"You always knew what to do, Grandfather," Iris whispered. "For birds, for me . . . Your instincts were so good and kind. I feel so lost now, so very lost. . . ."

Iris' spirits lifted when she found the blue granite stepping stones that led to the sprawling white spruce tree that sat, like the heart of the grove, at the dead center of the poplars. Her boots skipped along the foot-worn stones, her heart hammering in her chest in anticipation of seeing the familiar site.

With one white-gloved hand she brushed withered poplar leaves and spruce needles off the wrought-iron bench that sat at the base of the spruce. Then, with a sigh of contentment that blended with the song of the poplars, she dropped down. Habit made her sit on the left side of the bench. Grandfather had always favored the right side when they visited this spot, and she accommodated his presence, even now.

Her intention had been just to sit for a moment before returning to the carriage, but the bench was welcoming and familiar, and Iris lingered. She leaned back against the thick trunk of the spruce, rested her head, and closed her eyes. Tension leached from her body, and her shoulders dropped while her breathing slowed. It was so peaceful here, so serene and quiet that the glade could have been completely removed from the bustling city. If she did not know better, she could have been in the countryside, far from every little thing that plagued her now that the full four and twenty months specified in Grandfather's will were coming to an end.

It was almost impossible to believe that he had been gone for so long. Almost unfathomable to think that if she didn't choose a husband in a matter of weeks, she would be obligated to wed a rogue. If only the irksome Earl of Hampfordshire had not pulled back. He wouldn't have been a love match, true, but Iris had thought she might—no, would—have learned to love him. Eventually. Perhaps. If luck was on her side. Hopefully.

A moot point now, whether or not she could have loved the earl. He had made his intentions—or his non-intentions—perfectly clear. It was all for the best, because now, more than ever before, Iris was determined to find someone completely suited to her heart.

But time was slipping by so quickly! How to find the right man in such short order? How to find someone who satisfied her heart as well as her head? How to—

"Pardon me, miss. Is this seat occupied?"

The voice was deep, cultured, and with a hint of an accent of unfamiliar origin.

Iris' eyes snapped open. Her head came away from its resting place on the tree trunk, and she sat up straight. For an instant she stared at the man standing before her. He had his back to the lowering sun, and with what little sunlight there was peeking through the clouds, she could not see his features. She held a hand up, shielding her eyes, and studied the stranger.

He looked harmless enough, but she knew that counted not at all. Clad in a well-cut gray overcoat with wide lapels, trousers that broke over spit-shined black boots, and with his top hat held loosely in one gloved hand, he looked as decorous as any gentleman might.

"Pardon?" Iris hated the quaver in her voice. She cleared her throat, inclined her head, and said, "My apologies. I'm not certain I heard you correctly."

The man took a step closer, bringing him more clearly into view. Wide, dark eyes. A cleft in his chin. Neatly shaved and, now that he was nearer, the scent of something musky and exotic coming off his person.

It was his hair that caught Iris' attention the most. Flame red and, even with a generous slick of pomade bringing out its luster, somewhat unrulier than most gentlemen's hairstyles. While his features were certainly grown-up, beneath his untamable, striking mop the man seemed almost boyish.

"I'm the one who should offer apologies. I didn't mean to startle you, but I didn't know how else to attract your attention than by asking an innocuous question." His grin was inviting, and Iris could not help herself. She smiled back at him.

"That was your intention? To ask a harmless question, even if its answer was blatantly obvious?" She gestured to the empty space beside her with a flourish.

The stranger inclined his head, and Iris repressed a smile at the loosely controlled locks that bounced with the movement.

"Ah . . ." He shrugged and then captured her gaze with his. A mischievous gleam sparkled in his chocolate brown eyes. "So you've discovered my secret already. I thought to keep it hidden, but I daresay I'm no expert in the art of conversation."

Iris ignored the last and asked, " 'Secret'? So you're a man with a secret?" She gave a mild gurgle of mirth. In the back of her mind, Iris heard her own voice saying it was quite improper to be conversing with a strange man—unaccompanied and without adequate introductions having been made—but she chased the voice from her head. It had been far too long since she had had any harmless fun; the kind of inoffensive banter they were engaged in could hardly be condemned by polite society.

"I must admit to being both a man and a purveyor of a secret or two."

"Or a dozen, I'd wager!" A giggle escaped her lips, surprising her to her core with its unexpectedness.

"You are a very perceptive woman. Although I think it safe to say that most, if not all, men have at least a dozen secrets they struggle to keep. And if I may be so bold, I would think women also have their hush-hush characteristics. Even a skeleton or two in the cupboard, some of them."

She looked up with a small nod. "Yes, I'd allow that we all have our secrets."

Using the hand that still held his hat, the man gestured toward the empty side of the bench. He raised an eyebrow and asked, "May I? I know it is bold, but it would be much more conducive to conversation if I did not have to stand and look down at you. And it might save your neck as well."

What harm could come of it? She had already broken the rules of etiquette regarding conversing with strangers, so why not continue what was quickly becoming an entertaining conversation? Iris shrugged, then nodded.

The man wasted no time. He sat beside her, leaving a foot between their bodies, a gesture that Iris appreciated.

"Much better," he said smoothly. "Don't you agree?"

Iris murmured her agreement.

"Now, where were we?"

"I'm not sure we were anywhere," she replied. She jerked a shoulder upward. "Besides beneath the tree, that is."

"Beneath the tree . . . beneath the beautiful white spruce tree, you mean. I have always loved this spot. I miss it when I am not in London." His gaze swept up to the tree limbs above them. Iris watched as he scanned the long-needled branches, noting he seemed in no hurry to cut short his examination. Finally he looked at her. "Do you come here often?"

The question should have sounded silly, but he asked it with such seriousness, Iris immediately nodded. "I do. Or, I did. Used to, I mean."

His brows knit. "You did? Or you do? Which is it?"

She sighed and then let the words tumble out in a rush. "Actually, I used to come here all the time. Several times each week, mostly in the morning. But recently—well, not only recently, but for most of the last two years—I haven't been here as often. Hardly at all, really. It's just . . . it's just so . . ." She offered a shrug when the words would not come.

The man beside her waited for several heartbeats before he gently prodded. "It's just what? What changed that keeps you away from this magical spot?"

"My life. It's what changed." The desire to share her confidences with this stranger overwhelmed Iris. It would lighten her burden substantially if she could just share the clutter that filled her mind with someone who had no investment, no concern at all, in her life or future. She sucked in a quick breath and then went on. "My grandfather passed away nearly two years ago. He's the one who used to come here with me. For the longest time I couldn't bring myself to visit this spot without him. Then, this morning actually, I felt an urgent need to see it again. Just to come and walk beneath the poplars. To sit on this bench and enjoy the tranquility. Just to . . ."

"To be?"

How could he know how she felt?

"Exactly! Just to come and be, and feel the strength of the trees and the serenity of the park. I hoped I might be able to untangle—" Iris swallowed her words. Regardless of how much she wanted to share her load, this man was a stranger. She couldn't go on . . . could she? Surely she shouldn't . . . should she?

"Untangle what? Surely not your hair—that looks tidy enough beneath your bonnet. Or your bonnet ribbons—they don't seem to need any untangling," he teased.

Iris shook her head with a laugh. "No, my hair and ribbons are fine."

"What, then?"

"I can't tell you. In fact, I've already told you more than I should have." Out of the corner of her eye, she saw him wrinkle his brow. Iris sat up straighter and stared at the trees in front of them. She knew he desired more information, but she held back.

"Hmm, having second thoughts about talking to me, are you?"

His insight pleased her, but she continued to maintain a cool detachment.

He pressed her. "What's the problem? You can't say I haven't been a complete gentleman the entire time we have been acquainted, can you? I have kept my distance, maintained every decorous manner as to keep my actions above reproach, and, if memory serves me, I haven't committed any offensive, foul-scented breach of bodily etiquette. So, what exactly keeps you mum at this point?"

Heat warmed Iris' cheeks. He was completely on target on all counts. No, the only scent coming from the man was one that was far from foul or offensive.

"It should be obvious," she said, folding her hands in her lap. "We haven't been properly introduced. I shouldn't even be talking to you at all, not without the appropriate introduction. What would people think?"

He glanced around them, pointedly leaning forward into her line of sight to scan the trees. Then he sat back, put one ankle across a knee, and slapped his thigh. "Well, since there isn't anyone here to perform an introduction, I don't see that there's anyone present who would think anything untoward was taking place either."

"Humph." He had a point, but conceding it was not something Iris wanted to do.

"Ah, so we're stuck on the introductory phase of our relationship, then?"

"A chance meeting in the park cannot be termed a 'relation-ship'—not by any stretch of the imagination."

"Right." He paused, then said slowly, "But if we were to be introduced—"

"I don't see how." The interruption was impolite but made before Iris realized it was on its way.

"Humor me. Just let us say we were introduced, in a rather roundabout, not-entirely-average fashion. Would that be enough for us to continue this conversation? I do hope you will say yes, because I have to admit, I am enjoying this exchange im-mensely. I had not thought to find someone so pleasant and diverting sitting on this bench, and now that I have, I am disin-clined to terminate our discussion. So, what do you say? A ca-sual introduction—would that do?"

Much to her surprise, Iris was also taken with the unex-pected discussion. She dashed her chin toward her chest, a jerky movement that set the feather on her bonnet flapping. "It would."

He placed his hands on his chest with a smile. "Then allow me to introduce myself. I know that's not done all that often in these parts, but I've been away for a while, and where I've been, it's commonplace for two people to take it upon them-selves to exchange introductions."

Her head swiveled, making the feather flap still more en-thusiastically. "Where? Where have you been?"

A loud chuckle was the first reply she got. Then he said, "America. I have been in America—New York to be exact—for the past five years. Therefore, you see, I am a tad out of touch with the London scene, as well as the niceties that accompany it. Forgive me, please, and allow me to introduce myself. I'm Graham."

Graham. That was all? Goodness, but he *was* out of touch, wasn't he? Iris debated whether to tell him that his one-word introduction was highly irregular. Given the circumstances of the day, she opted for accepting his introduction as it came.

"It's a pleasure to meet you, Graham."

"And you are . . . ?" He leaned close, but not so close that she was uncomfortable.

Iris debated a second time. Giving him her whole name made her bristle. He was, despite his charm and seemingly harmless countenance, a stranger. Did she wish a stranger to know her identity?

She stared into his eyes, weighing her options. Finally, she relented. "Iris." It was better to give him just a tiny bit of her, wasn't it? It was, she decided. Especially since she did not plan to ever see this Graham fellow again. It didn't seem likely that they knew the same people. She hadn't heard of anyone who knew someone in New York, and something like *that* was bound to be common knowledge, wasn't it?

No, surely this was one of those once-in-a-lifetime encounters that was spoken of but seldom actually occurred. Except that now, of course, it was occurring.

"Well, Iris, it's nice to meet you. Now that we have been introduced, maybe you can finish telling me what you are trying to untangle. What is it that's got you all tied up in knots?"

"My life," she admitted. Now that it was out, there was less pressure in her chest and her heart. "My life is a tangled mess, worse than my hair or bonnet ribbons have ever been."

"What snarls things up for you?" He spoke with the calm assurance of one who seemed used to finding damsels in distress and solving their problems for them. "And what can I do to help, my new friend Iris?"

She turned and looked into his eyes. There was friendliness in his open gaze, and for a brief moment she believed Graham might be able to help her. Then the memory of her current state of affairs washed over Iris coldly.

"Nothing. There is nothing you can do . . . nothing anyone can do. I have to find something, and soon, or I will be forced to do something I definitely do not want to do. No, worse than that. I'll have to do something so vile, I shudder to think of it!"

"What do you need to find? Maybe I can help with that."

"A husband. I have to find a husband—fast. You don't happen to have one of those in one of your overcoat pockets, do you?" The jest came in gulps as a lump the size of a fist lodged in Iris' throat.

Graham shook his head. "I'm sorry, but I don't. Nothing but lint in these pockets, I'm afraid."

Chapter Five

Hold still, miss. This corset is too tight by far. I shall have to give it one more good tug to get it nice and secure." Emma Jean threaded the corset laces through her fingers, taking hold so tightly, Iris saw her knuckles turn white. The maid, smaller in stature even than Iris, who was considered petite in any situation, waited until Iris sucked in a deep breath. Then she pulled.

Every last bit of air in Iris' lungs came out in a great *whoosh* as she felt her ribs crushed by the offending undergarment. Her vision dimmed, then cleared as her body adjusted to subsisting on the small, shallow breaths she was forced to take.

In the past, Iris had never worn such a fierce corset. Before, she had been content with the figure she cut wearing a thin under shift for modesty's sake. Occasionally—but unbeknownst to Grandfather—she had misted down her shift in order to make a gown conform to her body more dramatically. But never in all her twenty years had she condescended to be trussed like a game fowl before roasting. Had Grandfather been around to witness her descent into the trappings—the truly constrictive trappings—of fashion, he would have shaken his head and told her exactly how much nonsense he thought the whole affair.

The current fashion climate favored unencumbered under-pinnings rather than strict corsets, but drastic times called for drastic measures. And these? They were drastic times.

Moreover, Grandfather's not here, Iris reminded herself as she concentrated on maintaining her footing in the suddenly warm room. She moved away from the heat coming from the fire. *I am forced to make myself as comely as possible, even though it is wholly uncomfortable, in an attempt to counteract Grandfather's error in judgment.* Her musing made her shudder, bringing Emma Jean instantly to her side.

"You're chilled! Why did you step so far away from the fire? Here, let me get you a dressing gown, so you'll be warm enough while I style your hair."

It was more expedient to simply allow herself to be drawn close to the hearth, beside which her dressing table—with its curling irons, hairpins, and other paraphernalia designed to make her look and feel beautiful—waited. Iris sat dutifully on the low chair before the mirror. She watched Emma Jean test one of the irons with a spit-wet finger before applying it to the long, thick tresses that hung down Iris' back. It would take time, the knew, before the maid finished her upsweep, so she closed her eyes and settled herself against the chair's tufted back.

She had not told anyone about her indiscretion in the park. There had not been time, really. Yesterday, when she had returned to the house, Grandfather's solicitor had been waiting in the drawing room. It was unthinkable that she attempt to slough off dear old Mr. Clark, no matter how much doing so would have suited her mood. When Ethel told her he awaited her return, Iris removed her outer garments as quickly as possible, handing the coat, bonnet, and reticule to the housekeeper in an untidy bundle. Then she had hurried to the drawing room, anxious to hear what the visitor had to say.

Mr. Clark's visit had been purely a peek-in sort, something Iris had long since grown used to bearing. The gentleman was like the rest of Grandfather's acquaintances. He had taken an overt interest in Iris' well-being and checked in regularly to, as Mr. Clark put it, "share a cup of tea." Ordinarily Iris welcomed his visits, but yesterday it had been difficult to chat as if she didn't have a care in the world when all she could think of was her unchaperoned assignation, innocent though it was, with the stranger in the park. Granted, he had told her to call him Graham, but that was a far cry from a formal introduction. For all intents and purposes, Graham was still a stranger. The idea that she had spent even a scant half hour chatting with him, alone and in a sheltered location, brought a naughty shiver up her spine. The event was far bolder than any other she had ever indulged in.

The desire to confide in Bridget and Catherine niggled at her but not loudly enough to entice her to share the meeting with them. What harm could it do to savor the daring memory for a while, hold it close and let it bring a touch of adventure to her otherwise-dull life? Besides, neither Bridget nor Catherine would approve of the meeting, however unintentional its occurrence. No, better to keep it to herself. That way no one could raise a breeze.

Emma Jean wielded hairpins the same way a fencing enthusiast brandished a polished rapier. Her zeal to keep Iris' curls in place brought a forceful jab with what felt like the millionth hairpin to Iris' scalp.

Iris tried to pull away, but Emma Jean—and the hairpin—followed her.

"Ouch!" When Iris reached up to rub her scalp, her lady's maid pushed her hand away with a small gasp.

"Oh, no, miss! You don't want to mess things up, do you? I have all the ends tucked up tightly against your head, and—"

"*In* my head, it feels like."

"Oh, no, not in your head, no matter how it feels. Trust me; your hair will not be falling down out of its style, no matter how many times you dance. And I expect, what with that gorgeous green gown, you'll be asked to dance every single time the orchestra picks up an instrument." The maid's fingers worked their magic while she spoke, and before Iris could protest a second stabbing pain wrought by another pin, the hairstyle was finished. Emma Jean took a step back, admiring her handiwork. "There," she said, a note of pride in her voice, "that's lovely. Now you're certain to outshine everyone else at the ball."

Iris smiled into the looking glass, catching Emma Jean's gaze with her own. She nodded her approval, murmured her appreciation, and wondered if the young woman could possibly be right in her assertion.

The dress was gorgeous, the hair utter perfection, but could Iris be the most attractive woman at the Fall Fete? Emma Jean's opinion was flattering, but surely it was colored by their relationship. Wasn't it? Iris rarely felt unsure of her physical attributes, knowing full well they were more than adequate. However, at this moment the prospect of walking into a crowded room on her own, with nothing more than a smile and wave of her decorated lace fan to bolster her, turned her stomach. A sour taste rose in her mouth, but before she could swallow it away, there was a knock on the door.

"Who could that be?" Iris clutched her dressing gown closed. She watched Emma Jean open the door, peek her head out into the hallway, and then reach out to take something. When the maid returned, she held a silver tray.

"A note, miss." Emma Jean proffered the tray, holding it steady while Iris snatched the cream-colored rectangle.

"That's strange. I wonder who would be sending a message at this late hour. Surely whatever needs to be conveyed could wait an hour more and be delivered in person. Don't you think so, Emma Jean?" Taking care not to get wax beneath her fingernails, Iris broke the seal and opened the heavy sheet of vellum paper.

"I wouldn't know, miss," Emma Jean murmured as she began to unbutton the long line of fabric-covered buttons that marched like a procession of green picnic ants down the back of the gown lying across the counterpane.

The missive quivered in her hand as Iris scanned the elegantly penned words. Her breath caught in her throat. Her heart hammered, and heat rose in her cheeks. Waves of shock swept over Iris.

My dear Miss Newgate,

I trust you have not forgotten my request that you save tonight's waltzes for me. I assure you that I have not.

I look forward to this evening's festivities and to the prospect of our becoming better acquainted. I know that is what your grandfather wished for us.

With the hope of increasing your pleasure over the upcoming ball, I offer as some small measure of my high esteem, as well as my fervent expectations for our blooming

*association, the accompanying floral offering. It is a token
of the anticipation I feel over what I am certain will be a
very enjoyable, highly entertaining evening.*

*With fondest regards,
James*

Iris looked up. Emma Jean was doing her best not to appear curious, but the way the corners of her lips twitched clearly demonstrated the lengths she was forced to go to in order to contain herself.

" 'Floral offering'? Do you know anything about a floral arrangement?"

"Yes, miss. The butler indicated there was . . . uh, a floral offering. Although he made it sound like it was, um, a bit more involved than that sounds." Emma Jean flicked an imaginary piece of lint off the skirt of Iris' gown. It was clear she was holding something back, so Iris pressed her.

" 'Involved'? Whatever do you mean, Emma Jean? Did the man send a corsage?"

"No, not a corsage."

"A nosegay? Or a posy, then?"

A stray curl loosed itself from beneath the edge of the maid's starched white cap when she shook her head hard. "No. Neither of those, miss." A twitter escaped, its shrill sound brief but grating on Iris' already-frayed nerves.

"What, then? A bouquet? Did he send a bouquet?" Iris demanded.

Emma Jean's gaze rose to meet hers. She shook her head again, letting a second wisp of hair loose. "Not exactly, miss. It wasn't—well, it wasn't only the one bouquet he sent."

Knitting her brows together tightly, Iris mulled over the words for a moment. "You mean he sent more than one bouquet of flowers with this note?" She held the note high and waved it before her.

"That's right, miss. The butler said the note arrived with three dozen roses."

Three dozen roses? And from a man with whom she had barely spoken!

Her heart tripped over itself for a moment as she recalled their brief exchange. The duke's fine appearance and refreshing forthrightness had made a favorable impression, to be sure, but could she ignore the air of scandal surrounding him?

She could not, she decided. She would move ever onward to find a more suitable mate.

Chapter Six

Lady Hargrove-Smythe's Fall Fete was legendary for a number of reasons.

First, it was the final event of the Season, and anyone who was anyone—and even a few who were desirous of being someone someday, even if they were still technically no ones now—attended.

It was the last chance for women who had not made a match for themselves during the busiest part of the Season to show the *ton* there was still time for them to find a mate, or at least the promise of the same.

Quite possibly the biggest reason no one who lingered in the city would think of missing the Fall Fete was that Lady Hargrove-Smythe, despite her absolutely impeccable background, was known for being a tad extreme, especially when it came to the Fete. Her decorations were the most exotic, her food too divine for words, and those she invited were sure to be decked out beyond imagining.

The Fall Fete was the perfect way to mark CLOSED to the London Season, and everyone knew it.

Iris skimmed a gloved hand down the front of her skirt. Her ball gown rustled beneath her touch, a sound like the whisper of leaves in trees. Immediately she recalled her secret adventure in the park, and the bloom in her cheeks would have increased had the warmth of the room before her not already affected her fair skin. She hoped her color was not high enough to attract undue attention.

She scanned the ballroom, looking for either Catherine or Bridget. Her gaze swept over the elaborate gowns and the elegantly appointed gentlemen who hovered near the lavish dresses like butterflies over flowers, not putting a face or a name to anyone. That could come later. For now, all Iris wanted was to find one of her closest companions, to feel a connection to someone—anyone—before she stepped into the swirling chaos that was in full swing in Lady Hargrove-Smythe's enormous ballroom.

"Quite festive, don't you think?"

Iris felt Lord Whitman's breath on her cheek at the same instant she was enveloped by the spicy scent of his cologne. She drew in a shallow breath, conscious of her restrictive corset, before she turned to face the one man she had hoped to avoid for a while.

"Yes, it certainly is," she allowed. Her gaze was drawn to his. She noticed the sparkle in his eyes and instantly felt the tug of attraction that those deep eyes brought with them. So dark and inviting and completely unlike any other man's eyes she had ever seen . . . the shade of cobalt, perhaps because of its unusualness, held her captive. When Iris realized their gazes had locked, she blinked rapidly. Almost as soon as the connection was severed between them, she longed to have it again.

Directing her gaze back to the dance floor, she added, "The array of colors is quite breathtaking, isn't it?"

"I find the color green—emerald green, in particular—to be most delightful."

She looked up at him to see whether he teased her, but his face showed no sign of amusement. The serious look in his eyes took her by surprise, bringing a flutter to her head that was akin to the feeling one got upon standing too quickly.

"I—I—well, I am glad that the color pleases you, Lord Whitman," Iris murmured. She dipped her head politely, accepting his compliment with the grace born of a lifetime of lessons. "There are many other lovely shades of ball gowns here as well." A wave of her fan indicated the dancers. "Don't you agree?"

"There are, but I would much prefer discussing something a bit more personal, if you don't mind."

Her heart skittered in her chest. *Personal?* Whatever could he have in mind?

Lord Whitman went on smoothly, as if he had not noticed her trepidation. "I hoped you would be comfortable enough with me by now to use my Christian name, rather than the more formal method of address you've employed. Really, Iris, doesn't *James* slide more easily from your tongue than *Lord Whitman*?"

"But . . . we've not been properly introduced! I cannot—I will not—address you thus. What would people think?"

How oddly like her encounter with Graham this was! Yet her heart raced in a way it had not even in the park.

"Why do they need to know?" He flashed a smile that nearly swayed her.

"Besides," he continued, "your grandfather would have gotten around to introducing us eventually. We both know that was his intention. Can't we simply pretend that he had done so before his passing? Who would know he hadn't, aside from you and me, that is?"

"As you say, I would know. And you, as well, although it is

obvious you do not mind skipping social graces when it suits you. I should never have received you unannounced and would not have done so, either, had you—had you—"

"Had I what?" His grin showed he knew precisely what she meant.

"Had you given me any other option," Iris finished, feeling warmer and more ill at ease than she remembered feeling in ages. What was it about this man that made her feel like a long-tailed cat in a room filled with rocking chairs? His reputation aside, just being near him gave her the collywobbles.

"I do not believe in providing options that do not suit my purpose," he said in a tone that underscored his words. Iris noticed the flash in his eyes as he spoke. It was neither frightening nor intimidating to her, although she could well imagine it might be to someone with something to fear. He went on with a resigned air, "And if you insist on a proper introduction—although I sincerely believe it to be completely unnecessary and a perfectly illogical waste of time—I will see that one is made. Give me a moment, please."

Feeling as if she was a character in a comedy, Iris watched through disbelieving eyes as the man wove his way through the crowd. When he reached Lady Hargrove-Smythe, he took her hand, leaned close, and spoke into her right ear. Anyone looking on might surmise they shared a confidence too delicate for the general public's ears. Much to Iris' amazement—and mortification—the hostess turned her head and looked directly at her. Then she and Lord Whitman began to walk toward her, Lady Hargrove-Smythe's hand tucked possessively into the crook of the charming man's arm.

Too charming by far, flashed through Iris' mind.

Had it been possible, Iris would have let herself be swallowed by the crowd. But it could not be done, so she merely stood her ground, grateful that her skirt covered her knees so no one could see how hard they knocked together. She was sure to have bruises on them come morning.

"Iris! How nice to see you tonight." Lady Hargrove-Smythe's cologne was suffocating, but her greeting, and the smile that lit her round face, welcomed. Iris dropped into a curtsey at precisely the same instant her hostess did. Then she smiled in return.

"I'm so glad you invited me," Iris replied politely. She gestured with her fan toward the room. "The ball looks to be a huge success."

"Yes, it does, doesn't it? It is such a pleasure to be able to provide an evening's entertainment." The high color in their hostess' cheeks shone through the thick layer of powder on her skin. Iris noticed there were lines etched deeply into the other woman's forehead as her gaze skimmed the dance floor. Iris wondered what could be on Lady Hargrove-Smythe's mind, but before she could conjure up an unassuming yet provocative question, the lines disappeared, and a smile changed the older woman's features.

Iris felt their hostess hid something . . . but what? The moment passed in a flash, leaving her no more enlightened than she had been before recognizing concealment.

With a great show of enthusiasm, Lady Hargrove-Smythe turned her attention back to Iris. "Iris, my dear, I don't think you've yet had the pleasure of meeting a good friend of mine. May I introduce you to Lord James Whitman, the Duke of Willingham? Lord Whitman, this is Miss Iris Newgate, of London."

The introduction sent tremors up Iris' spine. Before now, their alliance was mere speculation, but now that she had been properly introduced, the man was full and well a part of her life that could not be ignored. Could he?

Surely not, Iris thought as she inclined her head and curtsied. *I cannot ignore Lord James Whitman, this duke—this dangerous duke—any longer, can I? Oh, Grandfather, what have you done to me?*

There was no time to muse further. The duke bowed, then took Iris' right hand in his and brought it to his lips. With boldness that belied fashion, he placed a small kiss where her knuckles lay beneath her glove. Releasing his hold on her so gently she didn't realize he had let her go, he looked up and smiled.

"It is a pleasure to finally make your acquaintance, Miss Newgate. A very great pleasure."

"Your Grace." Her throat was tight, but she made certain to speak loudly and clearly enough that she did not give the impression of being flustered by the introduction. Iris hid the fact that her tongue felt glued to the roof of her mouth like a trout drying on a sun-heated pier, fixing her features as blandly as she could manage, given the sudden hammering of her heart. "The pleasure is mutual, I assure you."

Lady Hargrove-Smythe saved Iris from further conversation. She reached out and put her hand on the duke's arm. With a smile that did nothing to hide the manipulation behind her careless question, she asked, "I believe you were well acquainted with Iris' late grandfather. You were friendly with Lord Colin Stanton, were you not?"

"I was indeed."

The hostess went on, leaving Iris to watch closemouthed and silent as if she was in the first row of a play audience instead of part of the action. "The two of you had dealings together, didn't you? I seem to recall his saying that you had quite a head for business. Yes, I'm sure that's what Colin said, not too long before he passed on."

"How kind of you to recall that and to relate it to me." The duke captured Iris' gaze with his. With a small grin, he winked at Iris before turning his full attention back to Lady Hargrove-Smythe. "Yes, Lord Stanton and I were closely allied on many fronts. Especially in the area of . . . ah, in the business world."

"Well, that is as I expected, then." Lady Hargrove-Smythe looked distractedly around the quickly filling room. She inhaled sharply, cocked her head in an obvious attempt to see into the crush of latecomers near the door, and waved a jewel-heavy hand in the couple's direction. "I hate to introduce and dash, but as you are both already familiar with each other via dear, departed Colin—what a sweet man your grandfather was, Iris—I will leave you to your own devices. Ta-ta!"

In a last plume of cologne she was off, moving across the room with more grace and agility than her sufficient girth gave hint of. They watched Lady Hargrove-Smythe disappear into the crowd. Then the duke turned his full attention back to Iris.

"She does move with the speed of a Tattersall's trotter when she wants to, doesn't she?" His comment required no answer, so Iris kept to herself. He raised an eyebrow, then quirked his lip teasingly. "So now that the proper introductions have been made, I suppose we shall be free to take our amusement tonight. I had hoped you and I might, ah, get to know each other better this evening."

Iris stared up into the dark blue eyes of the man she barely knew but who was, unless she proved capable of formulating another plan, destined to have her captured in a parson's mouse-trap. Married, to this man she knew both too much and yet so little of? With the orchestra striking the first notes of a new dance and the gay sound of so many voices creating a vacuum that left Iris feeling as if they were the only two people in the vast ballroom, the idea did not seem half-bad. Not half-bad at all, really. The music could almost make her forget all she had heard of the man, all the salacious gossip and tongue-wagging accusations.

Almost but not entirely.

"There is more to life than amusing oneself." Iris hated sounding like a stick in the mud, but his assumption that she would fall right under his spell irritated her. She flipped open her fan, somehow mollified when he raised an appreciative brow at her finesse, and went on smoothly, "Moreover, there are a few matters we should discuss before we plow full on into the merriment."

Iris Newgate's insistence that they adhere to the constraints of polite society down to the last detail was both infuriating and amusing. James had come to imagine that she of all women, with her keen intellect and streak of independence, would not mind skipping a step or two—or three or four, for that matter— when it came to the rigors of introductions or social interaction. Apparently he was wrong, at least when it came to him. Her besting him on the point brought an inward smirk of chagrin, one that he hid from her view. It would not do to have the alluring creature before him think he laughed at her expense.

But her persistence in holding their exchange to the exact letter of propriety vexed him as well. Another time, perhaps, he would enjoy a verbal sparring match with her. Now, all he wanted was to pull her close and twirl her onto the dance floor.

James surveyed Iris Newgate with a new and growing awareness. He was surprisingly attracted to her, both physically and intellectually. That much was clear. But could he feel an emotional attachment to her, even given time? That was the true question. Given the nature of his existence and the secrets it obliged him to keep, forming any true sentimental feelings for

Iris, or anyone else, could prove very costly. It might even cost him his life.

Rather than dwell on something he couldn't change or a question he didn't have an answer for, James leaned close and worked toward securing that which would prove a diversion— for now, at any rate. Whatever the cost, he must convince her to dance with him.

" 'Matters'? What, pray tell, are these 'matters' of which you speak? I cannot imagine what I can have possibly done to vex you so soon after our introduction. Why, I have hardly spoken a word, and I certainly have not infringed upon your . . ." He cast an appreciative glance over her, taking his time looking over every facet of her person.

Iris watched Lord Whitman's gaze move from the ostrich feather tucked into the curls above her left ear, down the skin exposed by her décolleté bodice, to the full sweep of her skirt, and finally to the tips of her embroidered dancing slippers. He cleared his throat before he continued speaking. The sound was deep, but his voice, when he spoke, was soft and tender. "I have not infringed upon your person in any way, shape, or form. So I cannot imagine what can be so pressing that you and I need to have a discussion before enjoying the Fete."

Iris swallowed hard, the memory of words read and reread coming to her now. Months earlier Bridget had secured a copy of the anonymous, and somewhat scandalous, new novel *Sense and Sensibility, A Novel by a Lady.* In it, the character Elinor had at first appealed most to Iris. Elinor's yearning for a man promised to another defied her practical and conventional nature. Iris had found her need to pull sense when it was in short supply into her situation had been a trait she herself identified with. Nevertheless, after the Earl of Hampfordshire's defection, the cause of which had never been made known, Iris had felt more like Marianne—distraught over the actions of the scoundrel who had jilted her.

Feeling like Marianne, with her hand-wringing and helplessness, even for a short time, had not sat well with Iris. Her true nature was to be more like Elinor, calm and determined—even detached when the need arose. It would have been simpler to just smile back into the duke's handsome face and to forget the items bristling in her mind with the same biting annoyance as if they were burrs attached to her stockings.

Easier but not entirely satisfying.

She refused to be diverted by Lord Whitman's charm or heart-stopping good looks.

"Flowers. We need to discuss the completely inappropriate tidal wave of flowers you sent to me. Roses, of all things! They are far too extravagant a gesture for a man to make to a woman he had not yet properly met. Of course, I am appreciative of the blooms; they are quite wonderful and have brought great pleasure to my household. Thank you. But they are, still and all, a gesture that seems out of line with propriety. And the note. Let us not forget that, shall we? It was—well, it was . . . uh . . ." Her mind chose that moment to go absolutely blank. She stared up at Lord Whitman, hypnotized by the way his eyes sparkled in the glow of the room's lamplight and the kind yet amused way he waited for her to continue.

When the moment grew long, Lord Whitman shook his head with a smile. "As you have clearly received—and, I trust, read—my note, you are aware of my hopes for this evening's waltzes. And"—he cocked his head toward the dance floor—"if I'm not mistaken—and I know I'm not—those are most decidedly the first chords of a waltz. My favorite waltz, to be precise. Shall we, Miss Newgate?"

Without waiting for her reply, the tall, perfectly proportioned duke swept Iris into his arms and onto the dance floor. As she fell automatically into step with him, she realized that, for the first time ever in her entire life, she felt perfectly at home.

The feeling lasted for the count of eight beats before her mind pushed aside such nonsense, and a small measure of sense—as well as sensibility—returned.

Chapter Seven

Several hours later Iris, Bridget, and Catherine sat in a row before a wide mirror in one of Lady Hargrove-Smythe's second-story bedrooms. It, and several others like it, had been made ready for partygoers to rest and refresh themselves. The room they had chosen to occupy was farther from the ballroom than most, and the trio hoped to find themselves uninterrupted. This was their first opportunity to exchange confidences since the ball's start, and they did not want any distractions. Or, heaven forbid, overzealous eavesdroppers.

Catherine patted her golden curls with a careful hand. The spray her maid had liberally doused her locks with before artfully arranging them in the newest fashion was concocted using, in part, rosewater and heather from the Scottish moors. It was quite pricey but did the job of holding her coiffure in place with a minimum number of hairpins. Without the headache that invariably arrived when the hairpins on a woman's head grew so heavy that the desire to lie down came upon her, Catherine bubbled her pleasure over the ball's success.

"I would so love for Ethan to be here tonight," she sighed.

The hand-worked lace edging the neckline of her scooped bodice fluttered. Catherine's gown, made from the finest silk available, was sheer and, had it not been for the body-hugging under gown she wore beneath its periwinkle blue skirts, would have been nearly shameful. On Catherine it looked perfectly fetching, and she was the epitome of impeccable grace and flawless bloodlines. "How he would love the dancing! You do know he is a swell of the first stare, a highly fashionable man, and when he holds out his hand and makes a sweep with his leg . . . oh, I do say he outshines everyone else. Of course, he is a bit—a teeny, tiny bit, mind you—on the theatrical side, but what else would one expect from a man of his caliber?"

"What, indeed?" Bridget pulled a face, showing she believed Ethan Daniel Harding to be more than a "teeny, tiny bit" theatrical. To her credit, she did not try to hide her expression. Instead, she made a successful effort to catch Catherine's attention. When she saw she had, Bridget shrugged off her words, giving assurance with a sweet glance that she was merely teasing. "You are right; Ethan would love to kick up his heels to precisely the high musical standards he seems to enjoy most. It reminds me of that evening at Almack's, the night a fortnight or so before he left for his holiday—"

"Business tour abroad," Catherine corrected. It was a small matter of the vernacular but one she never failed to enforce. The other two supposed that *holiday* made Ethan's absence sound more like fun than Catherine cared for. They generally acquiesced on the point, only infrequently confusing the terms.

"That's what I meant, duck," Bridget pacified. Iris stifled a giggle; only Bridget could get away with calling Catherine that. "As I was saying, this music is on par with the music that night. Don't you agree?"

"You're right about that." Catherine nodded. She stopped

fussing with her hair and turned an earnest face to Bridget and Iris. "I cannot wait until Ethan's return. Truly, I count the days. I would love it if he could be with me tonight, and we could dance the night away with nothing separating us but his evening dress and this sheer silk. I wish . . . oh, I wish I could feel his breath on my cheek, instead of the cold emptiness of . . ." She placed a hand on her cheek and closed her eyes tightly shut. "Of nothing."

Catherine's longing made Iris want to reach out and give her friend an enormous hug. Bridget sat between them, however, so hugging was not an option for the moment. When Catherine's eyes opened, they held a sheen of unshed tears. Iris responded instantly, hoping to stem the crying that seemed so near to hand.

She said the first thing that popped into her head. Then she wished she could pull the words back and swallow them down, but, of course, that was impossible. Once they were out there, they were out for good.

"I met a man." Four words, in a rush, to divert an impending tear-fest. The intention was selfless. Why, then, did Iris feel as if she sat on a red-hot poker? Beneath the stares her declaration wrought, she grew warm.

"You mean you formally 'met' Lord James Whitman, the Duke of Willingham, don't you?" Bridget spoke slowly, each word having its own weight and substance. Her use of the man's full name, spoken as it was, made Iris fidget beneath their stares.

A line of perspiration broke out on her upper lip. It would be no stretch to nod and let the matter lie, but telling falsehoods, or even omitting the truth, was not Iris' style.

"Well . . . yes, of course I did meet the duke properly tonight. Lady Hargrove-Smythe herself made the introductions." *There.* She could change the subject and act as if that was what she had meant all along. But these were her dearest friends—her family, almost—and letting the dust settle around a half-truth wouldn't do. Besides, she needed their advice on yesterday's meeting in the park—even though she knew that the advice would be accompanied by admonitions.

Well, that could not be helped.

"I . . . well, I, uh . . ."

"Out with it, Iris!" Catherine had forgotten her own love worries. She sat on the edge of her chair and leaned forward. "You what?"

"I didn't mean the duke when I, uh, said I'd met a man. I met another man . . . not tonight, but yesterday. A different man," she finished lamely. Even to her own ears, she sounded vague.

Bridget called her on her vagueness. "You sound too smoky by half, my friend. We know you too well to let you slide on this. It is clear you are hiding something. Isn't it, Catherine?"

Catherine shook her head up and down so swiftly, it was a good thing she had been spritzed with imported, extra-sturdy hair-setting spray. None of her artfully arranged golden curls moved.

"I'm not hiding anything . . . not really. If I were, would I be telling you I had met someone? Answer me that." Iris defended herself as best she could, all the while knowing it was only a matter of time—minutes, but more likely seconds—before her companions learned the whole truth.

"We're not children anymore, Iris. Bridget's a married woman, and I am nearly so. You can't think we don't see that you're hiding more behind your fan than your face." Catherine furrowed her brows, giving Iris a queer stare.

"Fine. I will tell the whole story, but don't say you didn't ask for it when I do. And"—she held up a hand in front of her, cutting off the words that were about to tumble from the other women's opened mouths—"don't interrupt me until I'm done. If you do, I will stop right where I am and not tell you anything more. I want to tell the story, what little of it there actually is, straight through so we can head back downstairs. There is a ball going on, or hadn't you two noticed?"

Mutely, Bridget and Catherine snapped their mouths shut. They waited for Iris to tell her story. And, knowing the telling was not going to get any less difficult if she waited, Iris plunged right in.

When she had told it all, from beginning to end and leaving nothing out, the room fell silent. Both women openly gaped, their sentiments patently clear. They thought she was touched in the upper works, absolutely crazy for having done such a thing.

Catherine was the first to speak, her voice barely more than a whisper. "You'll be ruined if anyone finds out. Alone with a man you haven't been introduced to? In the park, beneath the trees in a secluded grove? Goodness, Iris, whatever were you thinking?"

Iris shrugged. Her shoulders felt lighter, as if the weight of what she had done had dragged them down to the level of her waist. Now they felt properly aligned with the rest of her body, and she was grateful she had told the story.

"I'm not sure I was actually thinking anything, to tell the truth. All I wanted was to find some peace and quiet and, I hoped, some answers to help me untangle the mess my life has become." She held out a hand, palm up. "I never would have guessed I'd be in such a bind. Never! But I am, and all I really wanted was to sit and think and to perhaps find a spot where I could feel Grandfather's touch and his wisdom. That's all."

Bridget *tut-tutted* before she spoke, her lips pulled into a thin, disapproving line. "What you found instead was a stranger, a man whose 'touch' could seriously affect your prospects for a good match. Catherine's right, Iris. You'll be ruined if anyone finds out."

"I know," she said with a sigh. No one would care that she had done nothing untoward with Graham. No one would care that theirs had been a chance meeting rather than a wicked conference. Her reputation would be tarnished, perhaps irreparably. "But I swear to you both that it is not as it seems. It was a chance meeting. I was sitting beneath the trees when he stumbled upon me. There was no underhandedness to the meeting, no well-laid plan. It was simply a chance encounter, that's all. I give my word."

Catherine snorted, the sound highly unladylike, more telling than words just how the news had taken her. "Your word? Why, that's not going to save your reputation, Iris. You can kiss your chances of making a good match good-bye if anyone hears about this. Oh!" Catherine slapped herself on the forehead with one fine-boned hand. Theatrics came to her after a fashion as well. She and Ethan were well matched. "The horror of it! If anyone learns of your indiscretion, you won't find a man to wed you—not now or ever. You will be a spinster, one whose prospects were ruined by a solitary blunder. Oh, Iris, I am so sorry! You know I'd rather stick my spoon into the wall than be a tabby—"

Catherine's flood ended as abruptly as it had begun. She slapped her hand over her mouth, her eyes so wide that they looked like milk saucers.

Bridget swept in, her words meant to pour oil on the waters. "Catherine didn't mean that, Iris. You know she sometimes speaks before she thinks—I believe it is that high-priced spray she coats her hair with. Some of it must seep down into her brain and cloud her thinking." She shot Catherine a disapproving look.

Iris slowly shook her head. No, Catherine was right. If anyone found out about what had taken place—even though nothing had taken place—in the park, she was done for. Being dead as opposed to being a spinster was extreme, but in the end they would basically mean the same thing. She would be alone, as she was now, with no hope of having a home and family—the two things she wanted most in the world.

"No, Catherine spoke the truth," Iris said softly. "I didn't think, and it could very well cost me my prospects."

Bridget reached over and took Iris' hand in both of hers. A hard edge came into her voice. "Then we'll just have to make sure no one learns of this . . . this . . . this silly breach of etiquette. You know that neither Catherine nor I will say a word. And as far as this Graham fellow goes—why, he is probably far from Town by now. You said you had never seen him before yesterday, so what are the chances any of us will ever set eyes on him again?" She stood, pulling Iris up with her. Catherine rose also, looking less jittery now that she had taken her hand away from over her lips.

"Bridget's right," Catherine said, her voice holding none of its previous shrillness. "No one will know, and we won't breathe a word. And that man, that Gr—that fellow you met—is probably miles from here already. Perhaps he has gone back to America." She leaned close and pulled Iris into a fast hug. When they separated, Catherine was grinning. "And good riddance to bad rubbish, I say!"

"Hear, hear!" Bridget held out her arms. They linked up and stepped toward the door. "Now, let's go downstairs and take a turn or two around the dance floor. Or, in your case, Iris, spend every toe-tapping minute whirling about. I do say, I think you've danced nearly every dance with that dashing duke of yours."

"He's not *my* duke. Yes, I have danced a number of waltzes

with him, and I have to admit, he is wonderfully light on his feet." It was true; the duke was divine on the dance floor. Had he not been, Iris would certainly have been footsore by now.

As the trio tripped down the wide staircase with broad smiles on their faces, her feet were the very last things on Iris' mind. And the duke? Despite her vows to the contrary, he occupied the biggest portion of her giddy thoughts.

She suddenly realized that she was happy. Not just an everyday sort of happy, but a real, down-to-the-tips-of-her-toes feeling of contentment. It had been so very long since she had felt this way. Iris prayed the wonderful feeling would last.

Almost before the last line of her spur-of-the-moment prayer was silently spoken, she saw a sight that made her mouth go dry. Blood rushed to her face as her heart skittered in her chest.

It couldn't be . . . could it?

It was. Just as Iris, Catherine, and Bridget neared the bottom of the staircase, the head holding the bright red mop of hair she had spied turned. Its owner looked toward the stair.

There was no place to hide. Iris felt like a small gray mouse cornered by the biggest, fiercest house cat in existence. She stopped dead in her tracks and watched as recognition dawned on his face. Then, to her abject horror, Graham smiled.

To add insult to injury, he winked!

His outrageous wink was the last thing Iris remembered seeing before her world went black.

Chapter Eight

Iris let the heavy brown velvet drapery panel drop back into place and turned from a gloomy view of the garden. She faced the room before her. Grandfather's library, with its floor-to-ceiling, wall-to-wall bookcases, had always been one of her favorite places in the house. Now, it oppressed her with its trapped-in-time atmosphere.

She looked around at the endless rows of expensive volumes. Many of the books she had read, some more than once. Instead of bringing her comfort, these old, treasured friends, their embossed spines stared accusingly out at her. She felt reproached for being here alone, without Grandfather. It was as if the books sensed that she did not belong in the library—let alone the huge house—without the charming, elderly gentleman.

Adrift. That was it. She was like a bit of sea glass, lost at sea without any hope of finding a home or someone to appreciate her.

Stop it! The stern reprimand filled her mind and brought her thoughts of self-pity and alienation to a halt. *This is ridiculous! I'm feeling sorry for myself, that's all,* she thought. A frown

creased her forehead. Self-pity, self-indulgence—they were
traits she could not tolerate in others. How had she come to
own such troublesome characteristics?

With a sigh, Iris lifted a framed photograph off a side table.
She ran a fingertip over the familiar face behind the glass and
felt instantly calmed.

"You were all I ever had," she said softly. Her grandfather's
likeness remained silent and still, but she heard his reply in
her head nonetheless.

*And you were all I had as well. We were a fine team, weren't
we, child?*

"We were, Grandfather. We surely were."

*Now I charge you with finding a new member for your team.
Find someone to love you the way you deserve to be loved. But
do not overlook the obvious, child. Remember, you are a Newgate, and Newgates do not settle for anything—or anyone—
but the best!*

"So I've heard, all my life." Her sarcastic tone was wasted
on the portrait. She set it back onto the polished table with a
thud. "But what if the so-called 'best' is about to take a tumble? Fall from grace because I was too silly and self-indulgent
to care how I presented myself? Botheration! Who could have
guessed that the trees wouldn't keep a secret?"

Thoroughly disgusted with her present situation and the
part she had played in bringing it upon herself, Iris strode
across the room. She sat down at the wide, mahogany desk, in
the comfortable, brown leather desk chair. She sat ramrod
straight, too annoyed to pamper herself by being comfortable.
Taking a sheet of writing paper from a top drawer, she gath-
ered her thoughts.

Before she could change her mind, she lifted a plumed pen

and dipped it into the inkwell on the desk. Then she held it poised above the writing paper.

"Well, look at you! All cooped up in this musty old place on such a day. Who ever would have imagined that the butterfly at last night's ball would fly back into her cocoon?" Bridget burst through the library doors with a swish of skirts, the heels of her shoes rapping against the floor like a string of gunshots. "Whatever are you doing in here, Iris? It's dark and gloomy, and your hair is pulled back so tightly, it's a wonder your eyebrows aren't touching your hairline!"

Iris touched the subdued knot at the back of her head. Bridget had a point; this morning Iris had scraped her hair back with such vengeance, it had hurt.

"Well, good morning to you too." Iris did not bother to rise in greeting; Bridget sailed into the room and dropped into the chair on the other side of the writing desk before it was possible to do so. As her friend settled herself, Iris moved her hand with the intention of placing the pen on the blotter and saving the writing paper for later. A large, wet blob of ink fell onto the paper's surface when she moved, leaving a mark that was too unfortunate to ignore. The paper was useless now, so she set the pen down beside the blot and sat back.

"What are you doing there? Making mud patterns on paper? Or perhaps they are renderings of horse patties, preserved in caricature for posterity?" Bridget leaned closer, pushing the edge of the sheet of paper with one delicate fingertip. The wet ink ran, giving the original blot three offshoots. "Now it looks like an octopus, doesn't it? Minus a few limbs, that is."

"Yes, it does look like an octopus. Not that I've ever seen one outside the pages of a book." She lifted her gaze to meet Bridget's.

Bridget wore an all-too-familiar expression on her face, one Iris recognized well, having seen it time and again. A plan brewed behind the dark eyes that stared back at her. Something was on Bridget's mind, and from experience Iris realized that her companion would not share her thoughts until she was good and ready to do so. Better not to try to pry out of Bridget something she was not ready to divulge.

Ignoring the tiny flutter of apprehension that flitted through her, Iris retrieved the notepaper from the blotter and crushed it in her hand. She tossed it into the leather wastebasket beside the desk, then leaned back against the smooth chair back and waited. Eventually Bridget would spill whatever secret she kept.

The wait was a short one.

"Have you heard the news?" Bridget adjusted the folds of the russet-colored embroidered skirt of her jaconet muslin walking frock. Watching her, it occurred to Iris that her friend had not waited for a carriage to be brought around to convey her on this visit, but had instead taken it upon herself to walk the short distance between the two houses. During brighter weather it was a pleasant, invigorating journey, but given the overcast day? Something very pressing indeed must have spurred Bridget on.

"News? What news? I haven't been out of the house all morning, so I have had no chance to learn news of any sort." What could have happened that was important enough to entice Bridget to ruin a hem with mud stains? Her fastidious nature rarely allowed for such behavior. Even when they were young, in pigtails rather than chignons, Bridget had been the one who was overly fussy about her appearance. She had never been reprimanded by her nurse or governess over a grass stain or, heaven forbid, a muddy hem. Iris couldn't wait to hear the earth-shattering news.

"And you have received no visitors?" Bridget pressed the issue, an inquiring lift to her chin. The warm-hued dress set off her complexion wonderfully, making her dark beauty show to its best advantage. Her color was high, and her eyes flashed, giving an air of mystery and suspense to the conversation. "No one besides me?"

"No, no one else. Why?"

Bridget nodded appreciatively. "Ah, so you really haven't been privy to the latest developments, then."

The wait irritated Iris. She leaned forward, put her hands on the desk blotter, and asked, "Whatever are you going on about? 'Developments'—aside from my making a cake of myself at Lady Hargrove-Smythe's Fall Fete, you mean? News in excess of my social blunder, my undeniable debacle, my descent into the lowest corners of the socially inept? News of more than my ridiculous behavior, my outlandish and irreconcilably embarrassing—"

Bridget's hand went up into the air between them, the same way a bobby might divert traffic.

"Enough! Enough self-pity and self-loathing, Iris. It is truly unwarranted and unnecessary. Good heavens, what woman hasn't swooned a time or two? Intentionally or otherwise? Really, you act as if no one had ever seen a lady pass out. Now, if anyone had gotten a good, hard look at that ridiculous corset you had tied yourself up in . . . Well, that would have been newsworthy. Really, Iris, whatever were you thinking to wear such a thing? And you, with such a comely waistline. It was an impractical move, and, honestly, I am quite surprised that you trussed yourself up like that. It is unlike you to be so vain. Whatever got into you?" She paused, giving Iris a long, thoughtful stare. Her hand had dropped to her lap when she began to speak. Now its fingers drummed slowly on the arm of the chair she occupied, their tapping making the moments seem counted by a time-piece.

"I don't know," Iris finally admitted. She looked down at her-self and knew that Bridget's assessment was accurate. Her waistline was smaller than either Bridget's or Catherine's, and while it would not be at all gracious of her to point out the fact, they were all aware that she possessed the most petite figure. "I don't know what possessed me to wear the outlandish garment. They should be outlawed, and those who sell them should be tossed into the dungeons—or, better yet, taken to the Old Bailey and duly executed for having committed such a crime against women." She giggled at the image of some unknown man—wearing the torturous device that had been blamed for her col-lapse the previous evening—facing the executioner in rare style. What a sight that would be—certain to draw a large crowd to watch the spectacle.

"Old Bailey? The executioner's hatchet? I know you're put out by your abrupt leave-taking from the ball, but doesn't that seem a trifle harsh? Truly, Iris, while you may have missed a few hours dancing, you still retain your head. Have you forgotten the whole eye-for-an-eye scripture? Demanding a fellow's head—on or off a platter—is stiff penalty for waist-cinching, I'd say!"

The pair laughed at the preposterous idea, their amusement lifting Iris' spirits enormously. Bridget had a way of making any situation seem less serious and more manageable. She was levelheaded, and that sensibility brought an ability to see through to the core of an issue.

Iris had let everyone believe that her restrictive undergar-ment had overcome her. It was simpler, albeit somewhat cow-ardly, to pass off her lost consciousness to the corset than to divulge the real reason she had keeled over on the staircase.

Even now, she wondered if she had imagined the cause for her untimely faint. Nevertheless, no, she knew she had seen what she had seen. She knew it, and yet she could not admit to anything other than having worn an ill-fitting corset.

All night long she had been haunted by the image of that head of red hair and the knowledge that beneath it lay the one thing that could bring about her downfall. Her ruination. Destroy any prospects she had of ever making a good match.

Still, Iris was far too fair to slough the entire weight of the situation off onto Graham's shoulders. She had to assume some responsibility for her position. After all, she had known right from their first exchanged word that to speak with him might be social suicide.

Bridget's voice cut through Iris' thoughts. "Well? Do you agree or not?"

"Agree? To what?" Iris had lost the thread of the conversation. She furrowed her brows, hoping to appear fully engaged.

Her friend was not fooled. She heaved a long, shuddering sigh. "Your head is in the clouds this morning, isn't it? I asked whether or not you thought it fitting that the man who designed the corset should have his head chopped off. Personally, I think the sentence is a touch excessive, but I'm not the one who so dramatically fell unconscious on Lady Hargrove-Smythe's staircase."

"I suppose you have a point," Iris allowed with a smile. She made a motion with her hand, miming severing her head from her shoulders. "I may be overreacting a tad."

"Glad to see you have still got your senses about you. But if you haven't yet heard the morning's news, you may be shocked senseless anyhow."

"Well, are you going to sit on the news like a hen on an egg, or are you going to tell me what it is that has you scooting over here without your carriage?"

Iris could not wait any longer. She wanted to know what the fuss was about—and now!

"There has been another murder!" Bridget said finally, her words coming out in a rush. She held up a hand, fingers extended, before her face. "Five. That makes five murders in the past six months."

The string of murders—all still unsolved—had marred this Season's festivities and had marked it as one of the most noteworthy in years. The first four victims had been low-ranking members of the peerage, all barons of such obscurity that their deaths had not been much more than fodder for idle conversation.

There had been hints, behind closed doors of course, at any number of suspects. Everyone was open to scrutiny, and wherever one went there was sure to be someone who could—and would, for entertainment's sake—cast aspersions or suspicions any and all ways.

More than once it had been whispered that Lord Whitman was behind the crimes, but that's all anyone did in that regard—whisper. No one had the gumption—foolhardiness, actually—to openly state their opinion that the man was responsible for such an underhanded activity. Still, a whisper here and another there added up. Wagging tongues were nearly impossible to still—not that Lord Whitman had made any attempt at all to still them. He seemed to regard such musings regarding a criminal aspect to his personality as complimentary.

"Another baron?" Iris asked, knowing full well that it must be. Had the murder victim been someone other than a baron, he would be exempt from Bridget's finger count.

"It was. Lord Pickering. I never met the man, so I doubt you have either, but I do hear he was a notorious gambler. Mayhap that is what led to his untimely demise . . . ?"

"Were the other victims gamblers as well?" The question was a silly one. There was hardly a man they knew, aside from the vicar, who did not wager now and again.

A fierce nod of confirmation. "Oh, yes—very high-wagering gamblers, I've heard."

The most important question sought escape from Iris' lips. "What time, do you know? Has anyone said what time this Pickering gave up the ghost?" She held her breath, praying the man had died while the ball was in full swing.

"Early this morning, apparently. Sometime well past midnight. I suppose anyone could be to blame . . . the Fall Fete ended shortly past eleven."

Chapter Nine

At least no one else has been murdered. It has been—what has it been now? Three weeks?" Catherine lowered her embroidery to her lap, cocked her head, and looked into the air, as if searching for the correct answer to her own question.

Iris exchanged an amused glance with Bridget. Sometimes their friend could be so completely empty-headed! It was a good thing that her heart was so large. It more than made up for Catherine's lack of common sense.

"Five weeks," Iris supplied. She stabbed her needle into the linen sampler she worked on, counting the space between where she was and the spot where the pattern's French knots began. She dreaded the intricate knots and wished she had chosen to work a piece without any knots at all. There was no help for it now; the sampler was nearly complete, and she would have to work the French knots, even if it took every ounce of concentration to get each and every one of the challenging little dots correctly aligned. She sighed. Her stores of concentration were low of late, her mind being so occupied with thoughts of the will's approaching deadline.

"Five weeks? Are you sure? It hardly seems it can really have been that long." Catherine's eyes opened wide, her long eyelashes fluttering in surprise. "Why, it seems like just yesterday we drew up a list of possible murder suspects, doesn't it?"

"Iris is right. It has been five weeks. Five weeks and a day, actually. Remember, Lord Pickering was murdered the night of the Fall Fete. That was on the first of November. Since today is the ninth of December, it is exactly five weeks and one day since the event." Bridget spoke without taking her gaze from her needlework. She was stitching a pillow cover as a Christmas gift for her mother-in-law and was adamant that it be perfect. Her mother-in-law was a notoriously fussy woman, and Iris doubted that anything Bridget gave her would ever be appreciated, but she kept that opinion close to her chest. The pillow cover was lovely, and it seemed a shame to waste it on someone who would not realize its worth or the hard work that went into its creation. "Time does fly, doesn't it?"

"On angels' wings," Iris muttered. Time's over-swift passing vexed her, haunting her dreams and turning them to nightmares. She had not gotten a peaceful night's sleep in so long, she could not remember the last time she had closed her eyes and not been too troubled for uninterrupted slumber.

Her time was running out—quickly. What had seemed an annoyance, an odd stipulation to Grandfather's will, was now a do-or-die situation. If she could not find a suitable man to do the marital walk with her, she might as well die rather than wed a man she did not love.

Lord Whitman had not called on her since the Fall Fete, although he had sent flowers—more roses—on five separate occasions. Each week since they had last seen each other, in fact. Again, he never sent one dozen roses, either. Every time it had been three dozen—a dozen each of white, pink, and yellow blooms. They were spectacular, and Iris had to admit that the gesture did bring him closer to being in her good graces.

Catherine resumed her sewing. She was working an intricate border on a length of aquamarine silk to be used in her bridal trousseau. While Catherine had never said precisely what the silk was to be used for and colored demurely whenever questioned about the piece's fate, Iris thought it probable that the aquamarine silk was to become part of a boudoir ensemble. She could not be sure, but it seemed likely that the border would make a beautiful addition to the lower hem of a bed jacket or dressing gown.

"Five weeks." A sigh escaped Catherine's lips. "Five weeks and still no clue as to the identity of the murderer. I suppose neither of you thinks we should offer our list of suspects to the authorities, do you?"

"No, I certainly do not think that wise," Bridget said quickly.

"Why not?" Catherine refused to let the matter drop.

Bridget looked at Iris with a "Can you believe her?" expression on her face. Then, speaking slowly, as if to a child or one with a mental deficiency, she said, "I am quite certain that the investigative authorities are capable of solving the rash of murders without any help from the likes of us. I believe such foolishness would only bring humiliation and embarrassment down upon our ears, my well-meaning friend. No one would take our list seriously. Besides, I bet that every name we came up with—barring my mother-in-law's—has been considered by the police. Moreover, I am fairly certain that those whose names were remotely plausible have been thoroughly investigated."

"It doesn't matter, anyhow," Iris said. She wove the end of the sky blue thread she was using through the last row of stitching. Then she reached into her sewing basket, pulled out a tiny pair of sharp embroidery scissors, and cut the excess thread. She poked her needle into a pincushion rather than rethreading it. It was too late to begin on the French knots. They could wait for a day when she was more refreshed than she now felt. "I threw the list away."

"'Away'?" Catherine parroted. "What do you mean, you threw it away?"

"I mean I crumpled it up and tossed it into the fireplace. Watched it go up in smoke, then out the flue. Is that a clear enough mind picture for you, Catherine? Honestly, whatever did you think we were going to do with that thing, anyhow? If the police cannot capture this criminal, then we surely cannot. Drafting that list was nothing more than an amusing way to pass a gloomy afternoon."

Bridget scowled at her stitching. It amazed Iris that Bridget ever completed a piece, so high were her standards. She watched as Bridget carefully removed a few tiny but obviously misplaced or misaligned stitches. Then she watched the furrow of concentration on Bridget's brow deepen as she replaced the unsatisfactory bits. After a few silent moments, Bridget's forehead eased, and she smiled.

As she wove the end of her thread behind her stitches, Bridget agreed. "Iris is right. That little list was just a silly game, duck. Honestly, sometimes you take the queerest things to heart!"

Catherine sniffed. "'Queer'? 'Little game'? I cannot believe you two would make fun and fancy from this horrid situation. Lord Pickering was the . . . What was he, the fifth or sixth man killed this Season?"

"Fifth," Iris supplied.

"Right, the fifth." Catherine carefully folded her silk, then returned it to the cotton bag she kept it in when she wasn't working on it. She bent at the waist, putting her supplies back into the small wicker sewing basket she had brought with her. She pushed the ivory toggle through a wicker loop, fastening the basket securely closed. Sitting up, she held out her right hand, ticking off names as she raised fingers to match. "Lord Pickering—he was the last one. I never met him. Before him, it was Lord Oliver. I never met him, either. The middle one was . . . Oh, let me see . . . He was the one with the odd name, wasn't he? Lord . . . Lord Stankman, that was it! Another on the growing list of barons I have yet to meet—or, in the case of these blokes, will never meet. All right, who was the second victim? Do either of you know, because I can't recall. . . ."

Bridget smiled as smugly as a cat with a canary in its mouth. "The second unfortunate baron was Lord Dashell-Pembroke. And I daresay no one met him. From what I can gather from my husband, Dashell-Pembroke was a recluse. Kept to himself, and had it not been for his one servant's wanting his wages, this mysterious baron wouldn't have been discovered dead for months— if ever. So, I believe you would be hard pressed to locate any acquaintance of the deceased Lord Dashell-Pembroke's."

Lord Miles, Bridget's husband, was an avid polo player. As such, he knew—or met, anyhow—more members of the peerage, as well as those connected to them, than most of his peers. It wasn't a shock to learn that he, of all people, had inside information on the baron.

Catherine raised a fifth finger. "And the first victim was . . ."

"Lord Byron. No one could ever forget that name, could they? Not a poet, this poor, dead soul, but at least his name affords him some measure of infamy," Iris said. She was a great fan of poetry and was more than happy that the victim had not been anyone famous, just someone with a memorable moniker.

" 'Infamy'? I would say that being the first victim of this scurrilous killer would be reason enough to garner infamy of some kind, however dubious its origin. But I see your point and your intention. It is bad enough that these five barons are dead, but at least they are remote members of society and not likely to be overly missed. If a baron of some standing in the community, someone with a gift for the arts or even the theatre, was to be murdered . . . Well, that would surely cause some upheaval, wouldn't it?" Bridget stared at Iris with pursed lips. She looked as if she had just licked a lemon. "Wait a minute. They were all barons, weren't they?"

"You know they were," Catherine said. "All five of them were barons, although barons of some obscurity, I'd say."

The meat of Bridget's musing hit Iris with some force. *All barons.* There had to be a connection, didn't there? Surely, it could not be coincidence that each of the murder victims held the same title.

"I see what you're getting at." Thoughts of the murders had plagued Catherine and Bridget incessantly, as their reluctance to discuss anything else attested to, but Iris had been too preoccupied with her impending deadline to dwell overmuch on current events. Until now, when a link between the victims began to clearly show itself.

Sometimes obtuse, Catherine raised and then lowered her slim shoulders. "I don't."

Bridget heaved a sigh, exasperation fairly dripping from her pores. "Don't you see Catherine? All of the dead men were barons. All of them. No dukes, or counts, or anything else for that matter. Just barons. Do you see now?"

"I do. But so what?"

Iris took up the thread. "Not 'so what'—more of a 'so why,'

I'd say. *Why?* Why kill only barons? Why not kill someone besides a baron?"

"Ah . . . now I see what you're getting at. You think there is a meaningful connection because all of the murdered men were barons and not someone else. Just barons—now I get it!"

"I knew you would, duck," Bridget said. She stared at her hands, absentmindedly twirling her wedding band around on her delicate finger. Speaking so softly that her voice was almost a whisper, she went on, "But the pressing question is, why? Why kill only barons? It is perplexing, to say the very least. Perchance the only way to discover the truth is to track down someone who knew all five victims, someone who was acquainted in some manner with each of those ill-fated men."

"That's a tall order." Iris knew it was an understatement. What were the chances they would find someone who knew all five men? None had been social, or fashionable, or any of the things that would bring him into the circles they knew. No, it was too remote a possibility to even consider.

"Don't I know it?" Bridget crossed her arms beneath her chest, looking resigned to discovering another route to learning more about the situation. "We'll likely never find someone who was acquainted with all five victims. We'd just as likely discover a squirrel wearing a top hat than find an acquaintance of all five of these distant barons."

Catherine could not contain herself. Her laughter startled the others. "That is an easy-enough request."

Iris blinked. "Pardon?"

"To find someone who knows—or knew—the dead barons is an easy task," Catherine said. She reached into the placket opening in her skirt and pulled out an embroidered lace hanky. She touched it to the end of her nose, then tucked it away again.

"I know just the person—someone who was fairly well acquainted with the men in question."

"Who? For goodness' sake, Catherine, who knew the dead barons?" Bridget's impatience was undisguised, her voice louder than was decorous.

Catherine shrugged her right shoulder. "Anne."

"Anne? Anne who? You know we are acquainted with at least six or seven Annes—which Anne do you mean?" Bridget sounded close to exploding.

"*Anne.* Lady Hargrove-Smythe. *That* Anne." Catherine's face glowed like a beacon. "Anne knew all the men who were killed. I heard her say so only a few days ago."

"Why didn't you say so before now?" Bridget's hand lay curled into a tight fist in her lap.

"You didn't ask."

Iris tugged the bellpull beside her chair, summoning the housekeeper. She rose, going to the desk to retrieve a sheet of writing paper and a quill. Carefully she penned a note. She handed it to Ethel, who had come into the room and waited silently for instructions.

"Would you please ask Jackson to take this to Lady Hargrove-Smythe's house? Tell him to deliver it and then wait for a reply. When one arrives, bring it to me as soon as it gets here." The housekeeper took the note, executed a fast bob, then left.

Within an hour's time, the trio had been invited to tea the following afternoon at Lady Hargrove-Smythe's home. Iris prayed the socialite had some answers to the questions most pressing on her mind. If she could fathom, one way or another, whether Lord Whitman was involved in the crime spree, it would make her decision, wedding-wise, much less complicated. If the man was only a rogue, she might be able to swallow the idea of marrying him. But if he was, as people whispered, a murderer? Then Iris would have to either find someone else in the very short span of time left to her or else figure out how to ask Mr. Clark, Grandfather's elderly solicitor, to marry her. Either way, she needed answers—fast.

It was her fervent hope that Anne would provide some.

Chapter Ten

The meeting was foolhardy, but when Lord Whitman's card had arrived, accompanied by a short note with his unusual request, Iris did not refuse him. Rather, she had provided a meeting time, as he had asked. Now she wondered, for perhaps the hundredth time, whether her acceptance of his proposed visit had been too hasty. Why hadn't she given more thought to his appeal?

Her hands were slicked with perspiration, but she didn't dare wipe them on the skirt of her lavender silk morning dress. Its intricately embroidered sarcenet overskirt was much too delicate to use as a towel. The room was warmed by the roaring flames in the deep fireplace, so waving her fingers in the air did nothing to dry them. Recognizing the futility of her damp-hands situation, Iris dropped her arms to her sides and hoped they would eventually take care of themselves.

The words of James' note, tucked away beneath her writing paper in the desk in her bedchamber, were etched into her memory.

My dear Miss Newgate,

I trust this note finds you well and enjoying the fine, brisk days of late fall. Your demeanor suggests you are a woman who appreciates the beauty of nature. I hope this is so, as I am also fond of the outdoors. I believe we may find common ground in our shared interests, with the hope of forming a much friendlier, more intimate association.

I wonder if you would find it convenient to receive me tomorrow morning. I sincerely hope you might, as I feel we have pressing matters to discuss, matters that concern the not-too-distant future.

I await your response with sincere anticipation. I must press upon you the fact that I have a plan to put before you that I believe will be of benefit to both our interests. I hope you are willing to consider my suggestion. It will be mutually advantageous, I assure you.

> *With fondest regards,*
> *James*

Twin blossoms of color bloomed on Iris' cheeks. She had lain awake most of the night, tossing around the various scenarios the infamous lord might have up his sleeve to bring before her. She hoped—for his sake as well as to save her the stinging hand she was sure to have after being forced to slap his handsome face—that his "mutually advantageous" suggestion was nothing improper.

The sound of heels in the hallway brought all contemplation to a halt. Iris stood transfixed as the double drawing-room doors swung open on silent hinges. Ethel, looking every bit the starched housekeeper but still not as impressive or straight-backed as Grandfather's longtime butler, Yeats, had been, stepped into the room. Yeats had passed away a scant four months after Grandfather's passing, and Iris had not replaced him. It seemed unnecessary; she had few visitors, and Ethel was more than capable of announcing them, something she proved yet again when she dipped into a curtsey and said, "Lord Whitman, miss."

He breezed into the room right on Ethel's heels, looking finely turned out in his gray pinstriped morning coat and knife-pleated wool trousers. The black riding boots that encased his feet told her he had ridden his own mount rather than arriving by carriage. The gesture pleased her. It was far more trouble to ride than to be conveyed across town.

"Thank you, Ethel. Please bring tea in a few moments." She turned to face her visitor with a little smile glued firmly onto her face. "Lord Whitman." Iris bent her knees, curtseying while he gave a proper bow. "Won't you please be seated?" She indicated one of the dark blue damask settees that flanked the fireplace. When he lowered himself onto one, she sat on the one opposite, carefully arranging her hands in her lap and hoping they were not still so damp that they left marks on her skirt.

"It is kind of you to receive me this morning." His voice was as deep as she remembered it being. At the sound of it, a small ripple of pleasure shot through her. "I was pleased to learn that you were not otherwise occupied. I know how time-consuming things must be for you now that your Grandfather is gone. Running this large house, as well as taking care of his accounts, must claim a great deal of your attention."

The conversation was not what she had expected, although she had not really known what to expect from this enigmatic man. So many topics had swept through her imagination; so many slants to this requested meeting had seemed plausible. This mention of running the household and dealing with

Grandfather's business affairs had never entered Iris' mind as possible topics of conversation. My, but the man was a puzzle.

"Actually, I ran the household before . . . well, before Grandfather passed away." It was true. Ever since she had been old enough to fulfill the obligations required to run a house of some size, she had done so. In the early days of her duties. Yeats, as well as her grandfather himself, had been her advisors. Eventually she had gotten the hang of things, and they had left her to her own devices. A good thing, too, because now, despite not having had an older, more experienced woman to show her the ropes, Iris knew what was expected of a woman when she came into possession of her own household. "And Mr. Clark, Grandfather's solicitor, takes care of the rest. Of course I manage the household accounts, but as far as the more far-flung aspects of Grandfather's holdings go, the barrister does that job quite nicely."

It was on the tip of her tongue to ask what—if anything—any of this had to do with him, but she held her biting comments in check. Mayhap he was simply making polite conversation, and if the topics he chose seemed ill advised, she did not want to point that out. This was a social call, wasn't it? She had agreed to receive him, so now it fell to her to be social, even if it was a trying matter.

He nodded his understanding. With one knee crossed over the other, Lord Whitman looked every inch the wealthy peer. He seemed perfectly at ease sitting across from her. Iris deduced—just by the way he looked as if he hadn't a care in the world—that his palms were completely perspiration-free. For her part, her hands were drying but doing so more slowly than a slug slides across wet grass.

Ethel brought the tea tray and set it on the table between

them. She gave a polite curtsey and then left, pulling the doors closed behind her.

For want of anything else to do, Iris removed the cozy from the pot and lifted the bone-china teapot. "Tea?"

"Yes, please. Just a dollop of cream, if you would." He waited while she poured, then prepared his tea. When she handed the saucer to him, their fingers brushed. Iris nearly dropped the cup and saucer, she was so startled by the feel of his warm skin against hers, but he snatched the beverage midair. Lord Whitman crossed his legs and leaned back, once again looking completely at ease. "Thank you," he said. With a polite nod, he raised the thin-rimmed cup to his lips and drank.

Rather than fall under his spell again by watching the way his mouth moved when he swallowed, Iris held out a shaky hand and offered a tray of madeleines. "Biscuit?"

"No, thank you. The tea is refreshment enough."

Good manners had been hammered into her since childhood and took over now. While she would have liked the man to explain his presence without having to ask him what he was about, it wouldn't do to sit mutely, staring at him as if she were a child looking upon a sweets tray.

Iris searched for a way to question him about his visit. She considered, then discarded, several roundabout methods of broaching the subject. Finally she settled on the direct route. It had always worked to her advantage in the past; she hoped it would do as well for her now.

"Lord Whitman," she began, twitching the edges of her lips into a smile.

"Please call me James," he said smoothly. The gleam in his eyes reminded her of sunlight shimmering on the ocean. "After all, we have been properly introduced. You haven't forgotten our introduction, have you?"

"No, of course I haven't forgotten. But I hardly think we are well enough acquainted that I can address you so . . . so familiarly." The protest was lame, but it was all that she could think of. There was no reason they should not use Christian names with each other. He was right; polite, socially correct introductions had been made, and no one would flutter an eyelash if they were to engage in familiar address.

Iris objected solely on instinct. What instinct, however, she did not know. The only thing she was sure of was that calling the man James had such a familiar feel to it that it frightened her. Dare she be bold enough to allow such close feelings with a man whose many mysteries ran tongues ragged?

He set his cup and saucer down on the table. Leaning forward, his hands clasped between his knees, he stared into her eyes. Once again, Iris was reminded of the ocean, with its deepest, darkest, bluest depths. And as before she felt that she could easily be sucked into the intensity of such eyes.

The sigh that came from him shocked her. It sounded pulled from his toes. She could not imagine that anything having to do with her, or with their association, would evoke such emotion.

"I know you are wary of me, Iris." He held a hand up between them, cutting off her protest. Her mouth snapped shut, and she swallowed her words. He went on as if she hadn't nearly protested his using her given name. "And I will call you by your Christian name, despite your misgivings. You demanded a proper introduction, and I procured one to satisfy your—and the rest of the *ton*'s, as well—sensibilities. I have behaved in a courteous fashion with regard to every aspect of our acquaintance. Asking you to call me James, and calling you Iris, is not only within reason but meets all socially acceptable standards. Don't you agree?"

She saw no way out of his inquiry, so she nodded. Now she knew how a mouse trapped in a corner by a cat must feel.

"Good. I hoped you would see this in a new light." He sat back, crossed his legs again, and resumed looking as if he hadn't a care in the world. The self-satisfied gleam in his eyes was, in the face of her growing recognition that his point was valid, not impertinent in the least. He had technically won the point, but Iris had given in gracefully.

Better to choose my battles, she thought with a wry smirk of acceptance. Hadn't Grandfather counseled her to fight only the fights that mattered most? This skirmish regarding forms of address was not noteworthy, so she chose to ignore it now that it seemed solved to their mutual harmony.

"So, now that we have reached some accord on the entire name-calling protocol, perhaps we will be able to devote attention to more pressing matters."

"Pardon?"

One time, when she was twelve or thirteen, Iris had accompanied her grandfather on a visit to a Mr. Peabody. Mr. Peabody was an importer of fine mahogany furnishings, some of which her grandfather wished to purchase. The man was originally from Australia but had taken up residence on Newcastle Cross Road. They visited him in his home rather than his place of business, as Grandfather had already chosen the items he wanted to buy from Mr. Peabody's collection. Iris had sat inconspicuously amid the strange, intricately carved furnishings in Mr. Peabody's home while the men discussed their transaction. Mr. Peabody's accent had made it nearly impossible for her to decipher what he was saying, or what his short, staccato words meant. Iris remembered feeling at odds with the situation, her equilibrium lost in the conversation that floated just above her head like low-hanging clouds.

That feeling was full upon her again now. Lord Whitman—James—had such a quick thought process that he could as easily have been a frog bouncing among lily pads as a conversational partner. Some moments Iris felt fully engaged in their exchange; others she felt lost. The effect was maddening.

Frustration made her words sharper than she intended. "What are you talking about?"

He looked surprised at her tone. In a voice designed, she was certain, to soothe rather than incite, he said, "Surely you know we have matters to attend to. Fairly urgent matters, if I do say so myself. Wouldn't you agree?"

No one had ever called Iris obstinate to her face, but she acknowledged the stubborn streak that ran, wide as a carriage lane through Nottingham Park, down her back. She squared her shoulders, unwavering in her desire not to be cowed by his unfaltering confidence.

"I daresay you and I have somewhat differing opinions of what constitutes a pressing—or, as you say, urgent—matter. Truly, I do not believe that you and I have anything much to discuss, Lord—ah, James. Why, we scarcely know each other. Whatever could we have between us that could possibly be so pressing?" When James opened his mouth, the answer to the question requiring not one whit of thought, Iris pressed on. It had been a foolish mistake to allow the man any opportunity to gain the upper hand in this little *tête-à-tête*. She would not make the same blunder again.

"More tea?" She picked up the teapot and, before he could protest, refilled his cup. He had only drunk half the cup's contents, so bringing the liquid to just beneath the delicate rim took a scant second. Iris deposited the pot on the tray, exchanged it for the plate of golden biscuits, and held the plate out to him. "A biscuit, James?" She smiled broadly, hoping to charm him into distraction. "Now, I hope you will not decline a second time. I know our Mrs. Perkins—oh!" The passing of time hadn't taught her not to say "our" anymore. A prickle of regret touched her heart, but she corrected herself and went on. A distraction should not be derailed by a—well, by a distraction. "I mean my Mrs. Perkins, my cook, takes great pride in her baking. I know how disappointed she will be if we send the tea tray back with her biscuits untouched. Surely you can at least taste one?"

James took a biscuit from her, then perched it on the edge of his saucer. "I make you nervous, don't I?" He cut off her denial with a wave of one hand. "No, please don't embarrass us both by saying it isn't so. I can see it in those beautiful eyes of yours. I can tell that my being here has set your nerves on edge."

Beautiful eyes? It is no wonder this man has such legendary success with women, Iris thought. Flattery tripped off his tongue with ease.

She watched as James took a bite of the biscuit and chewed it thoughtfully. The firm, chiseled line of his jaw and the way his mouth worked while he ate intrigued her. There was no disputing he was handsome. Or cultured. Or, as far as she could tell, restrained and respectful. Nevertheless, were those qualities enough to form a foundation for anything substantial or meaningful?

With a flash of dazzling white teeth, he smiled. "Your Mrs. Perkins has a right to be proud of her baking ability. That is one superb biscuit. Please, give your cook my compliments."

"Certainly." His admiration would bolster the cook's spirits a good bit. Since her master's death, there had been little call for an abundance of baking. Iris preferred fresh fruit to sugary treats. Catherine and Bridget rarely indulged in anything that might add to their waistlines, and as they were the most frequent visitors, Mrs. Perkins' baking utensils were nearly dusty with neglect.

He rose and stood before the hearth, leaning one elbow on the wide oak mantel. Unlike many houses in the area, this one was not ostentatious. It was a home where convenience mattered more than grandiosity, and function took precedence over pretentiousness. Somehow, the austere styling of the room was an ideal backdrop for the good-looking man. James appeared comfortable staring up at the painting above the mantel, as if he belonged in the spot.

He turned, and the intensity of the man slammed into Iris. His dark eyes searched hers, leaving her no room to hide her jumbled feelings.

"Let's not mince words, Iris. I confess I have no temperament for beating about the bush, no desire to play silly games with you. We are adults and should conduct ourselves accordingly." He studied her for a long moment. She saw he had a plan, but that was all she could tell from his serious expression.

She felt a sheen of perspiration appear on her upper lip, but she left it there, feeling too bare to expose herself further by a gesture as intimate as running a fingertip over her own lip.

"I will not shilly-shally any longer. Truthfully, my nerves cannot stand the experience," James said, softening his words with a smile. "I shall chance it and say you did not believe I had nerves, did you?"

"I believe you have nerves of steel." The answer was honest and more direct than most polite conversation called for, but the words escaped before she could close her lips around them.

James arched his eyebrows and then chuckled at her response. "Splendid! That is exactly the sort of spunk I admire in a woman. Finally, I have honesty instead of frippery from you, a reaction that is not ponderously weighed for politeness before it is given. I had hoped we could find this point in our relationship. I am somewhat surprised it has come this quickly and so easily, but I am not complaining. No, I am heartily pleased to find that you have as much fire as your grandfather indicated you possessed."

A stone tumbling from the top of a hill . . . that is what I am, Iris thought. *I am in motion and cannot stop, regardless of how much the mad journey sets me rolling!*

Words eluded her, so she watched as he came close to where she sat. When James sat beside her, the settee seemed dwarfed by his presence. She edged toward the padded armrest, hoping she did not appear frightened by him.

Apparently putting space between them did not put James off one bit. He took her hand in his and gently clasped it. His hand was warm and smooth, the fingers slightly calloused. It struck Iris as odd that a gentleman's fingertips should feel work-rough, but the thought flew from her mind when he spoke.

"I'll come right to it, Iris. I have a proposition for you—one that I believe will make life smoother for both of us. Your grandfather and I spoke at length about this before he died, and I know that Mr. Clark has apprised you of the contents of your grandfather's will. You know he approved of our marriage."

The cheek of the man! Iris opened her mouth to protest, but he cut her off with his next words.

"I propose that we carry out your grandfather's plan. I suggest you and I marry. And if it meets with your approval, I would prefer that the marriage take place as soon as possible."

James had expected Iris to be surprised by his proposal. Frankly, he might have been astonished by the matter as well, had he not been the one making the offer. If he had not had so much time to consider the options and weigh hers as well as his own, the idea might have seemed outlandish. But given the fact that somehow, some way, the woman had managed to pull him under her spell, impressing him with her beauty, grace, and brains, it was, he concluded, the only resolution to either of their problems.

He needed a wife, one he could trust and who would present herself with all the *élan* a woman of her social standing should possess. Iris needed a husband. It was not wasted on him that he was the default betrothal candidate once her grandfather's time limit had elapsed, but being the winner as a result of another's failure was intolerable. No, better to win through one's own merits, even if the heart being offered as a prize would not fully be his.

The harsh realities of life sometimes left little room for frills and rubbish. They needed each other, and unless she was too stubborn for words, Iris would see that too. He cared for her, more than he had expected to and more than enough to give her a decent life filled with all the things any woman might want. What they might lack in so-called true love, they would surely make up for in other areas. And who could tell about matters of the heart? Perhaps in short order, they would find themselves caring for each other in terms that were more romantic.

Moreover, if they did not find themselves so disposed, their marriage of convenience would fulfill more pressing needs than those of the heart.

Chapter Eleven

Iris leaned against a corner post of the massive bed in her room and wondered yet again how her life had gotten so out of control. She had never been unfortunate enough to be a passenger in a runaway carriage, but she imagined this must be how those stowed inside such a conveyance surely must feel. Life had been jostling her unmercifully these past months, and the symbolic bruises she wore were more tender than words could say.

How could James do such a thing? How on earth could he actually propose marriage?

Her stomach churned over the stampede of thoughts coursing through her mind. She ran one hand over her middle, hoping to calm her uneasiness.

This new twist might drive her to distraction.

She touched her forehead to the carved post and closed her eyes. The wood was cool to the touch and made the burning above her eyebrows lessen. A headache threatened, the throb of it still dull but strong enough that she knew it wouldn't take much to bring a thundering pain fully on.

An outing—that would do the trick. She should get out of

the house and find something—or someone—to better occupy her thoughts. There was no better way to chase away a headache than with a shopping trip, was there? Of course there wasn't! The day was young, and so was she, and allowing herself to become all out of sorts and headache-y simply because a man had popped a preposterous question was a supreme waste of time.

Feeling renewed, and with her head pain subsiding just a bit, she rang for Emma Jean. Now that she had made up her mind to do something, the wait for the maid felt interminable. Iris yanked on the bellpull a second time, then dashed to her closet herself. Why wait for someone else to gather her things when she had two perfectly good hands and was fully capable of doing so herself? She chose a favorite rose-colored morning dress, one she knew showed her complexion and figure to their best advantage.

Emma Jean raced into the room, her cheeks awash with color and her breath coming in great gulps, just as Iris dumped the dress, matching bonnet, and walking shoes onto the bed.

"Miss, are you all right?" Emma Jean's gaze swung between the bed and her mistress' face. "It isn't like you to ring more than once. I was helping Mrs. Perkins in the kitchen when I heard your call. Before I could properly dry my hands, you rang again, and we both grew concerned. Truly, miss, are you all right?" The concern in her eyes sent a pang of regret through Iris.

"I'm fine, and I apologize for worrying you. When you see Mrs. Perkins again, please let her know all is well." Iris unfastened the hooks at her neckline, pushing aside the hair that had fallen from its pins at the nape of her neck. She got the top ones open, but her arms weren't long enough to continue down the row on her back, so she turned, showing the maid what she needed done. Emma Jean rushed over and began to unfasten the dress. As she felt it begin to slide down her shoulders, Iris continued, "I have decided to go out. I have some shopping to do, and since the day is young and the weather unseasonably warm, I think a few hours out-of-doors will do wonders for me. Now, let's get me dressed so I can get to the shops before the noon hour."

Iris scrambled into the dress she had chosen and then sat impatiently while Emma Jean twisted her hair up into an artful chignon. When her hair was set, she swiveled on the stool, turning her head right, then left, in order to examine her appearance in the looking glass.

The face staring back at her from the mirror looked like the one she had seen every day of her life, but the emotions swirling about inside her belonged to someone she didn't know, to someone she had never met. Common sense told her that she was unchanged from the person she had been her whole life, but the unexpected turn of events that had taken place a scant hour earlier had left her feeling very unlike the woman who had wakened this morning in this very same room. How could it be that one experience could result in such complete and utter inner turmoil?

Get hold of yourself! Iris demanded silently. Her hands bunched into fists at her sides, clutching the material of her frock so tightly, she was surely leaving creases. She calmed herself with great effort, slowing her breathing until it came in an almost-normal rhythm.

She glanced at the ormolu clock on the mantel above the fireplace. Ten minutes before eleven. Plenty of time to get to the shops before it got too late. Her gaze dropped lower, and she saw that, while the drawing room had been the site of unprecedented uproar, the rest of the house had been running as orderly as was its habit. The grate had been freshly blacked, and although the fire was not burning at the moment, a full bucket of coal sat on the hearth, ready to chase away the coming afternoon's chill.

"Let us go before time gets away from us, Emma Jean." Iris grabbed a shawl a deeper shade of rose than her dress, as well as her reticule. "I am not sure what it is exactly that I need to purchase, but Grandfather always did say that an impromptu shopping expedition worked wonders for my disposition. And now, I assure you, my disposition is in dire need of a wonder . . . or two or three. So, let's not tarry."

She swept from the room and headed for the stairs. Emma Jean wordlessly followed her. No matter that the servant had kept her comments to herself; one look at her face as Iris passed her by was telling enough. It was clear that Emma Jean agreed that a shopping spree was in order.

The change dropped into the bottom of her reticule with a small jingle. Iris pulled the drawstring tight and looped the accessory over her wrist. Then she took the glass bowl of persimmon ice off the counter and turned to find an unoccupied seat. The clear, cloudless sky with its hint at warmth had brought shoppers out in full force, and the sweets shop was nearly packed full. Emma Jean was in the grocer's, picking up a tin of white sugar for Mrs. Perkins, so Iris only had to search for one seat. Still, a crowd had formed at the counter, and it blocked her view of the far side of the room. She cast her gaze about and found one empty chair at a small table near the front window. The table's other occupant was a white-haired matron, so Iris headed in that direction.

"Is this seat occupied?" she asked politely when she reached the table. The older woman looked up, shaking her head as she did.

"No, dear, it isn't. Feel free to make good use of the seat, and the table as well. I am about to take my leave, so this oasis in the midst of this madness will soon be all yours." When she smiled, it was clear that she had been a beautiful woman when she was younger. Now time had taken its toll on the friendly face, and creases indicated that the woman's life had not been all fun and frolic. "Pleasant weather we are having, isn't it? For so late in the year, that is."

The requisite weather chatter provided a safe, polite exchange. Iris took a tiny spoonful of the icy confection, savoring it on her tongue before she swallowed.

"Quite pleasant, actually. I was very grateful to see that gorgeous blue sky this morning, instead of the usual gray gloom that we are so famous for."

"I do know what you mean. I assure you, my old bones were thankful that the chilly weather is at bay, for today at any rate. I am quite certain that clear blue ceiling we were both so tickled to see was equally pleasing to our fellow shoppers." The woman nodded at the throng flooding into the sweets shop. "It seems we weren't the only ones with a treat on our minds today, dear."

"Apparently not." Iris cupped the bowl of persimmon ice in her hand. It was delicious, but she hoped to melt some of the ice crystals so that she could spoon it up with more ease. She changed gears and moved the conversation away from the weather and to the treat that had brought them to share the table. "The persimmons are quite sweet this year, don't you think?"

"Uncommonly sweet, I would say. I must admit, I do enjoy a lemon ice on a hot summer day, but the persimmon has been my favorite since I was a young girl." The glow in the other woman's eyes gave weight to her words. Iris watched as memories brought a new beauty to the woman's smile and thought again that the lady must have been stunning when she was in her prime. "Oh, but I digress, don't I? You did not ask for a trip down memory lane, did you? You were only making polite conversation, commenting on the sweetness of the fruit. Silly me, to drag you into my past. You must excuse my lapse. I hope you will indulge an old, lonely woman, my dear."

Setting her spoon down into her ice, then placing the half-consumed bowl of goodness on the polished marble tabletop, Iris shook her head. She wished she had not just filled her mouth while her dining partner spoke. It took a moment for her to swallow and then catch her breath.

"If you'll forgive my speaking my mind . . ."

The woman waved a gloved hand between them, urging Iris to continue. "Please, by all means, speak your mind, young lady. Not only to me, but also to anyone else you may chance to meet. Good heavens, we are of a time where women should be heard, I believe. We are out of the eighteenth century for real and for good, so let us take full advantage of the privileges— what few there are of them—available to us. Please, say whatever it is that is on your mind. Then, if you do not mind, I will share something with you."

Briefly, Iris speculated on what it could be that this new acquaintance could have to share with her. Then she did what she asked leave to do; she spoke her mind. After the crazy morning she had already experienced, how much more drama could voicing her opinion—even to a stranger—get her into?

"I just wanted to say that while I can't know about your loneliness, I have been in your company long enough to know that, whatever your chronological age, you are not an old woman. Not by any stretch of the imagination." Pleasure shone on her companion's features, making her steely gray eyes sparkle brightly. The expression impelled Iris to continue. She warmed to the topic. "I don't believe age—old age or youth—can be accurately measured in years. Oh, certainly, it is a jumping off point, but it is not—it cannot be—an accurate representation of wisdom or maturity. Can it?"

Rather than answer Iris' question, the woman asked one of her own. "And how old are you, my dear? Chronologically speaking, of course."

Sucking in a breath and holding it for a moment before she slowly released it, Iris contemplated her answer. She wasn't a ninny; she was perfectly well aware of how old she was. But in her heart? Or her mind? Sometimes she felt as tender as a toddler, other times, as ancient as the banks of the Thames.

"How old do you think I am?" She ventured to put forth the question, a slight tremor in her voice. "What age would you think I am, given our short acquaintance? And, please, answer honestly."

Her companion sat back against the wooden chair frame and stared straight into Iris' eyes. The look was probing, and for a moment Iris felt like an insect under a botanist's scrutiny. She squirmed, just a bit, in her seat, fearful that the face she presented to the world told more about her than she knew herself.

A smile, warm and encouraging, brightened the careworn face across from her, and Iris relaxed. "You, my dear, have one of those graceful faces that hides its owner's age so artfully and with such panache that you are a mystery. Yes, a mystery of the highest caliber, one that every onlooker wishes to own and one that has the capacity to drive men to distraction. You, my new friend, have the face—and evidently the intellect as well—of a woman to whom age is an afterthought rather than a defining issue. In short, you are timeless."

Speechless, Iris stared across the table for a long moment.

"Why . . . why . . . I don't know what to say! You are much too kind. I am flattered, but I assure you, there is nothing mysterious about me. Why, I am as open—and as readable—as any book, I am afraid."

The woman threw her head back and laughed. The sound was melodious, the notes tinkling like those from a well-played harpsichord. When her amusement subsided, Iris' companion reached into her reticule and pulled out her card. She pressed it into Iris' hand, giving her a squeeze before pulling her own hand away.

"That is my card, my enchanting new companion. I am more delighted than I can say that you and I have stumbled upon each other. I pray you will call on me sometime soon, so that we may speak again." She stopped, glanced out the shop front's wide window, and then turned her attention back to Iris. "And, if you recall, I mentioned that I wanted to share something with you. Do you remember that, my dear?"

With a quick nod, Iris murmured, "I do."

"Good. I hoped you did." Again she shot a look past Iris, into the street beyond. When her gaze met Iris' own, she leaned close and, in a voice barely above a whisper, said, "When we do meet again, I hope that you will enlighten me with regard to the gentleman who follows you." Iris opened her mouth to speak, but the other woman waved a dismissive hand and went on speaking, almost as if she had overstayed her welcome and was in a hurry to depart. "Say nothing, my dear. I know you are unaware of the man who has been watching you from across the street. That is why I am telling you now that you are, in fact, being followed. And it would seem to me that only a woman who possesses an air of mystery and intrigue would be someone a deliciously handsome gentleman like the one outside would find worthy of pursuit."

Forcing herself not to look out the window, Iris smiled as her dining companion rose to her feet.

Before she turned away, the other woman gave Iris a pat on the shoulder. It was a familiar gesture, one her grandfather had shown her countless times. An unexpected lump filled her throat. She blinked back a tear and smiled instead of crying.

"You have been far sweeter than the persimmons, my dear. Now, remember, I would love it if you would pay me a call. Please say you will."

How could she refuse? "I will try. I promise."

"Good enough. Good-bye for now."

Iris watched the crowd swallow her new friend. Then she waved when the woman emerged onto the street and got into a handsome, highly polished black cabriolet. As the carriage moved away, Iris glanced down at the calling card clasped in her hand: LADY SEFTON.

What? Who would have thought that one of the patronesses of Almack's might be out sampling persimmon ice?

Iris looked outside, her gaze searching the strip across the street from the sweets shop. There was a crowd, but eventually she saw a man leaning against a pole as if he had nowhere else to go and nothing more urgent to occupy his time. Her heart hammered in her chest as recognition sank in.

Graham, the man from the park. He was the one Lady Sefton had insisted was following her.

Suddenly the morning, even with its unexpected proposal, seemed quite tame.

Chapter Twelve

A week had passed since the unanticipated marriage proposal. Iris' suitor had not called again, but his admiration was quite clearly shown. Enormous bouquets of flowers of all kinds arrived every morning. Roses, of course, but other, more exotic and out-of-season blossoms arrived as well. Lilies in every color. Tulips, red and yellow both. Violets in delicate nosegays that reminded Iris of balmy summer days. In addition, irises— they arrived in abundance. Deep purple and all blooming to perfection.

As he had promised before taking his leave, James—for that was how Iris had come to think of him, in the Christian manner he had so strenuously solicited—had not shown himself on her doorstep but had left her to consider, at her leisure, his offer. He had given her his word he would provide all the time she needed to come to a decision about their betrothal, and she believed he would do just that. When he had assured her she could take her time and fully weigh the pros and cons of what he had put forward, the look in his cobalt eyes seemed sincere.

James had given her enough to think about that there were

times she thought her head might explode from thinking so hard. Grandfather had provided the best tutors and extensive schooling for his ward, so she was a woman completely capable of making up her own mind, but nothing in her lessons had prepared her for this.

There had been other offers of marriage. Several, in fact, in the months following her coming out. The men who had expressed interest had been nice and from good families, but none had made Iris feel giddy, and that was what she wanted to feel when she thought of marriage. She wanted to be swept off her feet, to have her heart hammer in her bosom and feel her tummy tremble at the sound of her future husband's voice. None of her previous suitors had had that effect on her, so she had turned them all down.

Now that she was on a tight schedule, one that would influence her entire future, and had to either find a marriage-worthy man or agree to wed the infamous man named in Grandfather's codicil, that very same man had gone and muddied the waters by making her decision even more difficult. He had insinuated himself to such a degree that when his daily floral tribute arrived, her pulse quickened and her stomach fluttered as if it held a flock of butterflies captive.

Catherine and Bridget had been quite put out when she had arrived home after her meeting with Lady Sefton to find them waiting in the drawing room. The visit with Anne Hargrove-Smythe, upon which they had all placed such high hopes of learning more about the murders and the dead barons, had flown completely from her mind after James' shocking morning proposal.

A mad dash to her dressing room and a quick change of clothing made her presentable for calling at the Hargrove-Smythe home, but while Iris' outer countenance proved satisfactory, her mind was engaged elsewhere. Thankfully, Catherine and Bridget had kept up a steady stream of conversation and filled in where Iris left huge, gaping blanks in their chatter. The visit yielded nothing by way of discovering who was behind the current crime spree. Evidently Anne was as flummoxed by the string of dead peers as everyone else and had nothing to offer by way of explanation.

Between thinking of James, and his marriage proposal, and her own pressing need to secure a husband or be forced to marry the selfsame man, Iris gave little thought to anything else. She lay awake nights, surrounded by the cloying scent of so many delicate blossoms, and pondered her situation.

The outcome looked the same, regardless of whatever so-called choice she made. Unless some other man danced into her life and claimed her heart, she would be forced to marry James. The prospect of marrying him grew less unsavory with each passing moment. Truly, he had been completely charming every time they met. Warm, witty, with a sense of humor, and handsome as well . . . What more could any woman want?

Love, Iris thought. So many marriages were arranged for financial, social, and familial reasons that love in and of itself was not the only issue at stake where marriage was concerned. She, like every other marriage-aged female, knew that. But still, she had always dreamed she would marry for love. Given the truth of the times, however, she might be able to set aside the criteria that her betrothal be precipitated by matters of the heart if something else were given in exchange for love. There was only one thing that she could think of that would be a fair exchange. . . .

Trust. Iris could marry a man she was only fond of—not in love with—if there was trust between them. Unfortunately, James inspired feelings that she could not completely cancel out as simply the first stirrings of a romantic nature. His eyes, those gorgeous cobalt eyes, hid something from her. She just knew they did. And, combined with the dead barons cropping up all around them, the idea that the man she was considering marrying concealed something of importance from her brought every leaning toward accepting his proposal to a screeching halt.

It might be better to accept James' offer, if only on principle; becoming betrothed because of a legal agreement, when there were no other worthy prospects in sight, would rankle her for the rest of her life.

Still, how could she possibly say she would marry a man who might be responsible for leaving a string of dead barons in his wake?

Iris had thought so long and so hard over the situation that it made her head ache. As she acknowledged the dull pain between her eyes, however, she was forced to confront an ache of an entirely different manner: the ache in her chest, in the vicinity of her heart. She had no idea what that particular pain might mean. She only knew that it was there—and growing stronger with each day that passed.

His lifestyle demanded that patience play a huge part in his character. James could be as still as a tabby cat waiting for a dormouse to pop its head out of its hidey-hole when he had to be, when situations regarding his political and professional leanings made the virtue essential. But waiting for an opportunity to present itself or a foe to tip his hand was drastically different than wondering when a woman would give an answer.

This was the first time in his life that James had waited more than a few minutes for any woman to grace him with a response to any request he made. He felt like a fish on a hook, dangling above the water's surface while the one who had snagged him debated his future.

The feelings coursing through him, the sort of which he had never experienced in the past regarding any proposition he had tendered, filled him with more apprehension than he cared to admit, even to himself. However, it seemed perfectly acceptable that any man who faced the parson's mousetrap might feel unsettled.

With too many emotions roiling within him to name, James strode from his desk to the liquor cabinet set in one corner of his study. He slid aside the ornately carved wooden door and reached inside. The wine decanter he pulled out was full. It was not his habit to drink to excess, so the wine, as well as the other bottles stored in the cabinet, was there for visitors.

James took a goblet off the shelf, and, wine bottle in one hand and goblet in the other, he walked across the room to sit in his favorite leather chair before the fireplace. The chair was rump-sprung from his spending so many hours in it, but, as this was his relaxation spot, he refused to allow it to be repaired or replaced.

Deep in thought, he settled into the chair. He poured a measure of the deep burgundy liquid, leaned back, and contemplated his future. With or without Iris, his was going to be a complicated life. He was embroiled much too deeply in his current affairs for it to be anything but complex. There would always be thorny issues for him to skirt, intricate matters demanding his attention, and life-or-death decisions to be made. He was accustomed to living on the edge, used to being beholden and accountable to no one save himself. Recently he had allowed his thoughts to include Iris Newgate in the mix, and now that she was affixed in his mind as part of his future, there was no shaking her out of it.

More to the point, James no longer wanted to push thoughts

of a future with Iris Newgate from his mind. He wanted her in his head, as well as in his life.

Is there no way for me to reclaim my mind? he wondered. *Surely to be this befuddled over a tempting armful must mean only one of two things: either I have been bewitched, or I have been touched in the upper works.*

With a snort of annoyance, James lifted the goblet to his lips and downed its contents in one swallow. If he was to have a headache, there may as well be a good reason for it.

Chapter Thirteen

The musicale was sparsely attended, being that there were so few fashionable people left in Town, but those who did attend made up for the light crowd with more laughter, applause, and merriment than was generally shown during the height of the Season.

At first, Iris balked at attending the entertainment so near Vauxhall Gardens, but Bridget and Catherine had insisted she come along with them. Even Anne, the epitome of delicate manners, agreed that there was no harm to be had in the evening's show. Finally Iris capitulated, and now that she was in attendance, she was glad that she had done so. Being out, surrounded by men and women in their finest attire, their only thought merriment, lightened the somber, contemplative mood that had enveloped her for days. She had not planned to be overwhelmed by her circumstances. It had happened as forcefully as a wave crashing over her at the seashore, and, like the full power of the ocean's fury, once the mood had swept over her, there was no trouble-free method of escape. That is, until tonight's festivities.

Iris applauded, her white-gloved palms muting the sound of

her pleasure. The harpsichord player was talented and made the oft-solemn notes of the heavy instrument sound uncharacteristically like bells tinkling on a careless breeze. She had lost herself to the notes of the piece, drawn into a world where nothing but sound mattered. It had been delightful, but now that it had come to an end, she was brought back to reality by a very real—and quite pressing—need.

Leaning over and using her fan to hide her face, Iris spoke softly to Catherine. "I shall be back shortly." When her friend moved as if to rise, she put a restraining hand on her wrist and shook her head. "No, it is all right. No need for you to get up. I just need to make a small detour to take my comfort. It will only take a few minutes. I'm sure I will be back before the next musical presentation."

A flash of understanding passed across Catherine's face. "Ah, I see. Are you certain you don't want me to come with you?"

Had there been a larger crowd, Iris would have instantly agreed to a companion for her personal errand. But since there was hardly anyone in the hall that they did not know, it was entirely unnecessary. Besides, Catherine was not one to move swiftly among a crowd, even one as meager as this, so taking her along would mean the trip would be lengthier than if Iris went alone. Conscious of her growing need, the decision to leave Catherine behind required no real thought.

"I am certain. Thank you for offering, but I shall be fine on my own. As I said, I'll be back before you even know I'm gone." She stood, arranging her skirts around her legs and adjusting her gloves so they were tight on her fingers. Even with needs to attend to, it would not be seemly for her to go off half-turned out. When she leaned down and picked up her beaded reticule, she whispered into Catherine's ear, "Be back in a tick. Or two, if there's a crowd."

There was no crowd at all to contend with. After she took care of her immediate needs, Iris lingered before the mirror. The room where the music was being played was warm, so she was rosy-cheeked. She pushed a stray lock of hair back into place near her temple. Then, satisfied that she was fit to be seen in public, she left the room and headed back downstairs to the music hall.

"Oof!" Iris turned a corner and collided with a solid form. The exclamation, as well as the air in her lungs, forced its way past her lips. For an instant, she saw stars, but, as firm hands reached out to steady her when she swayed, she quickly regained her wits. Her mouth opened a second time, with a dressing-down on the tip of her tongue, but before she could say a word, the man she had run into spoke. And when he did, the wits she had just managed to retrieve threatened to flee yet again.

"Please forgive me, Iris. I had no idea you would be coming around the corner so quickly. I saw you leave the music hall and hoped to meet up with you, but you are much faster than I thought you might be."

James looked down at her, an easy grin on his face. He was dressed smartly, as usual, in a meticulously tailored dark gray tailcoat, coordinating waistcoat, and pressed black trousers. A starched white shirt set off a midnight blue cravat that brought out the color of his eyes beautifully. He looked wealthy and self-assured, and despite her having found her footing, his hands stayed firmly on her upper arms.

A realization of his nearness as well as the strength and warmth of the hands upon her person came over Iris. It brought extra warmth to her cheeks, heat that had nothing at all to do with the temperature of the music hall.

"I . . . uh, yes, I suppose I am somewhat fleet-footed when

the need arises," she said. She felt a warm flush of embarrassment over having been observed leaving for the comfort room rise from her neck to cover her cheeks. She attempted to change the subject. "I . . . um, I did not notice you in the music hall. Were you here for the harpsichord pieces? And did you enjoy them?"

They were in the way of foot traffic, so James released his hold on her arms and, with the grace of one who had done it countless times, threaded her hand over his extended arm and led her away. Iris noticed they were strolling toward the wide, open double doors that led outside, but, short of planting her feet and refusing to move, there was little she could do but allow herself to go with him.

The first cool drafts of fresh air brought relief to her heated cheeks, so she was glad she had not put up a fuss about going outdoors. Besides, what harm could there be in standing just beyond the hall's doorway while they chatted? Others were doing the same, scattered in small bunches or pairs on the wide, square patio.

"I was there, standing in the back of the hall," James said. He placed his hand over hers where it lay on his arm, and the coolness that had so recently found her skin dissipated. "I was, unfortunately, delayed, so my arrival was such that I didn't wish to disturb anyone's pleasure. I stood, rather than create a stir, although I noticed an empty seat near you and would have greatly preferred it to my position near the door."

No witty reply came to mind, so Iris smiled up at him, hoping her expression was not so transparent that he could see how greatly his comment pleased her. Regardless of her growing feelings for the man, she refused to fall helplessly under his spell and throw herself at him like some Bird of Paradise or, worse, a Haymarket ware. She wasn't of easy virtue and had no wish to present herself as anything other than an elegant, well-bred lady.

Iris fixed her gaze on the sky behind James' head, snapping open her fan and using it to conceal the lower half of her face. She fanned herself slowly, annoyed that the stars were obscured by the glow from lights in the city. The crescent moon would have been lovely if the sky had been darker.

He noticed her skyward gaze. "Beautiful, isn't it? I admit, one of my greatest weaknesses is my fondness for the night sky. It is a vice of sorts, I suppose."

She snapped the fan closed with a giggle. "Stargazing? You?"

With a pained glint in his eyes, James placed his free hand over his chest in the vicinity of his heart. The put-upon, scandalized pantomime was unexpected, and funny, and looked completely out of place, especially in his evening finery. Iris giggled a second time, captivated by the way his handsome features had taken on boyish charm.

"I hear the sound of surprise in your voice, and I am, quite honestly, astounded. It is unconscionable that I have given the impression that I am not the kind of man who enjoys the simple pleasures the world has to offer. I love all aspects of nature . . . animals, country life, and, of course, the constellations. When we become closer, you will realize just how deeply matters of the earth affect me." He glanced up at the sky again, then down into her face. A smile, so brilliant the stars faded, made Iris' pulse race. So, too, did his next words. "Until we are, ah, more intimately acquainted, you will just have to take me at my word."

The innuendo was not lost on Iris. She was young and a bit naïve, but she was not stupid.

If he noticed her pulse quicken at his words, he gave no indication. James went on effortlessly, "Is astronomy an interest of yours, as well?"

She shook her head. "Not at all, I'm afraid. It was one of the areas that Grandfather and I did not investigate. I must confess that while I do enjoy looking up and seeing the twinkling lights, I cannot tell one from another." She grinned. "But I do know all the words to 'Twinkle, Twinkle, Little Star'—does that count toward being astronomically gifted?"

With obvious delight, James threw his head back and laughed. The sound carried on the night air, turning heads in their direction. Iris paid the curious onlookers no mind, relishing the opportunity to see his face lit up as she had never seen it before.

"Well, it does count for something." James began to meander along the walkway, drawing her along with him. "And since you have such a keen mind and an apparent aptitude for all things stellar, I'll give you a small introduction to the heavenly bodies above us by way of one of my favorite constellations. Let us just move away from some of the gaslights. They make everything seem so much duller, don't they?"

She opened her mouth to protest, but they were already several paces from the crowd. James pointed upward, and she fixed her eyes on his fingertip before she followed the path indicated. He was right; the stars were clearer here. Glittering like the diamonds of the children's song, they looked much closer now that they were not touched by the glow of the lights. With every step they took, the stars brightened.

"Do you see that constellation? The one that looks like a somewhat flattened *w*?" He pointed, but all she saw were stars. No letters from the alphabet anywhere. She shook her head. James stopped walking and took a step back. When he stood behind her, he stretched his arm out over her shoulder beside her head. "I know I am standing closer than is strictly proper, but it is purely in an educational slant, I assure you. Now, follow the line of my finger. Straight up, then to the left a ways. Do you see it? A *w* that looks like it's been squashed beneath a child's boot heel?"

Iris sucked in a deep breath, inhaling a tantalizing mixture of night air and the spicy cologne James wore. The mingling of scents relaxed her, and she disregarded his nearness in the hope of seeing that which seemed blatantly obvious to the man behind her. Her gaze scanned the black umbrella above, moving from one point of light to the next. She tried in vain to connect the glittering dots, her exasperation and frustration growing with every failed attempt at finding the elusive letter.

Then, success!

Joy, so pure and uplifting, swept through her. Not bothering to conceal her excitement, Iris pointed, her gloved fingertip touching his. "There! I see it! Right there, next to that big blurry bunch of stars."

Dropping his hand to his side and stepping away to stand beside her again, James nodded. "That's it—you found Cassiopeia. Another time I'll tell you about the cluster beside it, but for tonight let us focus our attention on one constellation." He tucked her arm into his and began walking again. "Cassiopeia is one of my favorite constellations."

"Why?" There were so many from which to choose. How could James pick favorites when they all shone as brilliantly as the Queen's diamonds?

He shrugged. "A few reasons, I suppose. First, it was one of the constellations I first learned to recognize without any help. My grandfather pointed it out to me when I was about six, and ever since that night I have been able to find it on my own. The joy of discovery really made an impression on my young heart."

Imagining James at six, and with a young anything, was nearly impossible at this moment. He was so mature, without a doubt completely grown-up, walking beside her that Iris' mind's eye refused to conjure a picture of a young James.

"Were you close to your grandfather?" A pang of longing touched her. Nearly two years—a heartbeat in time, yet it felt like an eternity since she had heard her own grandfather's voice.

As if he sensed her sadness, James squeezed her arm with his hand. He felt warm and solid beside her and pulled her back to the present moment. She appreciated the gesture, not wanting to mar the evening's pleasure by bringing sad thoughts to their conversation.

"I was. Very close, actually. My father . . . Well, my father was away a great deal, so I was left with my grandfather for long stretches of time. I did not mind in the least—I never felt deprived, believe me. He was a good man and took wonderful care of me."

"What about your mother?" It was a straightforward question, but she instantly wondered if it hadn't been too pushy.

James answered with a wave of his free hand. "She died when I was born. I never knew her, other than to know I was the one who killed her."

A chill shot up her spine. She shivered, gooseflesh rising on her arms. "You can't believe that, can you? You cannot possibly think a baby being brought into the world can be held accountable for an unfortunate medical outcome?"

He stopped walking and turned to look into her eyes. She saw there, even before he uttered a word, the answer to her question. The bottom dropped out of her stomach at the pain she saw so clearly etched his expression.

With so much conviction she did not dare broach an argument, James said, "Yes, I do. I have known my whole life that I was the cause of my mother's untimely demise. I killed her just as surely as if I'd run a knife through her heart. It seems that even before I drew my first breath, I was branded for life—marked a murderer from the moment of my birth."

She was too stunned to reply. Her feet moved automatically when he resumed their stroll. Emotions roiled through her like a winter stew set on a high flame. She was so close to bubbling over that it was hard to keep her emotions inside. Anger, disappointment, sadness. How could anyone—anyone with any conscience or heart—let a child believe himself capable of murder? Especially when the victim was the child's own mother! It was almost too dreadful a thought to bear.

They walked in silence for a few minutes, each deeply lost in concentration. Then, speaking as if the matter of his mother's death had never arisen, James continued her education on the constellations.

"Cassiopeia has a lovely legend attached to it, if you would care to know more about the grouping." The night air was cool, but Iris was not chilled. Enough heat transferred from James' nearness that she felt perfectly comfortable with him. The stars were sharper now, in direct contrast to the black tapestry to which they were affixed. Iris noted they had walked a good distance from the crowd. She could still hear murmured voices, so she did not feel completely cut off from all activity.

"I would love to hear it," Iris said truthfully. Then, wondering if his intent had been for her to decline his offer, she hurried to add, "That is, if you would not mind telling it to me. I am sure you have probably told the legend countless times. . . ." She trailed off, not willing to give voice to the thought that he had more than likely told endless streams of women this same exact tale. Still, she wanted to hear it, even if all her curiosity got her was a place on a long list of ardent listeners.

A fast quirk at the corner of James' mouth showed he knew what she was thinking. Hating her see-through appearance, she pulled her eyebrows together as if she was busy considering the idea. Then she nodded. "Yes, I would definitely like to hear the legend surrounding Cassiopeia, but don't feel put upon to tell me if you are bored with the tale. I am sure I will be able to find a volume on astronomy at the Avalon Road bookshop."

"I've just told you that it is one of my favorite constellations, Iris. As such, the legend is also one of my preferred stories." He paused, as if gauging the reception his words would garner. Leaning close enough that his breath touched her cheek, he said, "And what could be more pleasurable on such a beautiful fall evening than to tell a treasured tale of love and beauty to a woman so beautiful that she could charm the stars from the very heavens?"

Iris let out a little gasp, but James pretended not to hear it.

"So, the story of Cassiopeia . . . She was a great beauty, married to a king, and should have been, by all appearances, one of the happiest women anywhere. Cassiopeia and the king had a daughter named Andromeda. She was just as extraordinarily charming and beautiful as her mother. Cassiopeia's one fault was that she was boastful, telling all who would listen that her daughter was the most stunning creature alive. Well, as you can very well guess, not everyone liked being reminded ad nauseum about another's beauty. Poseidon became angry and sent a monster to kill Andromeda."

"How horrible! It wasn't the daughter's fault that her mother was a gabster and did not know how to hold her tongue. Why should she die because, through no fault of her own, she could outshine everyone else?" Indignantly she raised her gaze to the sky. Now that she knew how to find it, Cassiopeia fairly jumped out at her. The legend brought life to the grouping of stars.

With a deep, throaty chuckle, James said, "Fortunately for Andromeda, someone else thought the very same thing."

Thank goodness! "Who? Who realized the injustice of it all?"

His gaze was thoughtful. "Does it matter?"

"Of course it matters."

"So the 'who' of it is as important as the story itself? It's not enough that someone—a hero who saw her for who she truly was, who saw beyond her startling beauty to the intelligent, charming, loving woman hidden beneath the glossy exterior—came to her rescue? Does it really matter so fully the man's identity?" James held his breath and waited for her reply.

She thought it over but only for an instant. The truth was written on her heart. "Yes," she said quietly. "It matters."

"Why does it matter so greatly? I always assumed it was enough that the hero came rushing in, saved her from death, and that they lived happily ever after. I didn't realize that anything else, especially not the man's true identity, was of any importance."

"It is important. Can't you see that?"

He remained stubborn and steadfast and gave his head a forceful shake. A curl fell over his forehead, making him look even more debonair. Iris' fingers itched to push it back into place, but she curled her hand tightly into a fist and willed it to stay at her side.

She struggled to explain what, in her mind, needed no explanation. "All the things you say are important. She should be saved, and she should have a full, rich life—but with the right man. Don't you see? She cannot be saved by just *any* man. It should be the right man. The right man for her. She must be saved by her one true love, the hero who is hers and hers alone. It isn't a question of being saved; it is more a matter of fate, and of finding the exact match for one's heart. So yes, it matters greatly who saved Andromeda." She stopped, pulling in a breath and gazing into his eyes. They were dark, hidden by the shadows of the night, and unreadable.

Iris wondered if she had said too much, been too forceful with her opinion. Grandfather had chided her when she was a child for speaking her mind as if it were the gospel truth. He had said she didn't leave room for anyone else's opinions when she was convinced she was right. The trait to speak so forcefully was one she had curbed, but tonight's discussion sent her efforts at self-control tumbling to the paved walkway beneath her feet.

"Don't you see that?" she asked softly, appealing to the romantic side of him. She knew there was one lurking beyond his public persona after hearing his telling of Cassiopeia's legend. Only a man with a tender spot in his heart could spin such an enchanting tale.

James lifted her chin with a fingertip so that her face was tilted toward his. "Yes, I see. I see much more than I ever did before, Iris. Much, much more."

He caught her lips in a slow, gentle kiss. When he pulled back, Iris leaned toward him, all reason lost in the thrill of his touch.

More of a gentleman than he was generally credited for being, James did not immediately kiss her again. Instead, he traced a lazy thumb across her lips and whispered, "Yes, darling. I see so much more in so many things than I thought possible. Mostly I see sides of me that I did not realize existed. I don't know how you're doing it, but this rogue is falling under your spell."

Pulling her close, James kissed her again, with more intensity this time. Iris felt his heartbeat against her chest, felt the firm touch of his mouth on hers, and she was swept into a whirlpool of glorious sensations. She felt weightless, warm, and secure and imagined they were tucked up on one of the brilliantly glowing stars in Cassiopeia's cradle.

Without warning, a bloodcurdling scream filled the night air. Startled, James and Iris pulled apart, their eyes wide. Before either could speak, another scream issued forth. Then another.

A stampede of feet, heading toward where they stood, made James take a step back. The distance between their bodies was adequate for propriety's sake, but Iris felt suddenly cast adrift and wished she were still safely in his arms.

The woman who had loosed the initial, unintelligible scream began to wail. Her words were more frightening than her screams. "He's dead! By all that's holy, that man is dead— and just lying here in a puddle of his own blood, close enough to hear the musicians' work, had he any life left in his poor soul!"

They went with the crowd, following the woman's voice. Iris held back, having no desire to see the actual body in the center of the onlookers. She listened to the comments filtering through the crush.

One such comment chilled her to her very bones. James tightened his grip on her elbow, but he needn't have done so. She was rooted to the spot, too stunned to move. Then the man standing directly in front of them turned and caught her stare.

A sad shake of his head sent his gray mustache shaking. "Another baron. By blazes, another dead baron!"

Chapter Fourteen

Sleep was an elusive bedfellow and had danced well beyond James' reach all night long. Finally he had thrown on his dressing gown and, not inclined to wake any of the household staff, gone down to his study on silent feet. Ashes smoldered in the hearth; a brisk poke and two small logs had been sufficient to bring it fully to life. Then he had settled himself beside the fire, a snifter of brandy on the side table and enough to occupy his mind that he could have sat and pondered for days.

Botheration! Another dead baron—and right beneath his nose! *The London Daily Gazette* had yet to hit the street, but he could already guess what the headline would read. The powers-that-be at *The Daily Gazette* were wise enough not to point any journalistic fingers directly his way, knowing full well that his solicitor would be on them like the print on their paper. They would, however, find a roundabout manner of implicating him in the crime, bringing him further social scrutiny. His peers would talk, speculate, and even twitter behind open fans and upheld palms, though they would not approach him to either refute or confirm the gossip.

Well, notoriety had its benefits. One, the one that mattered most to James, was the dubious distinction that, while not bringing anyone to run openly from him, it inspired enough apprehension that made those who wondered about him keep their distance. And distance made his job less complicated.

James tapped his right forefinger against his temple. He stared at the tips of his house slippers, saw the neatly shined leather, and knew that his valet had given them recent attention. Hastings, the man who had cared for his clothing and dressed him since James had been in short pants, was but a flash in his mind. Thoughts of footwear led to memories of the previous night. And those? They, naturally, led straight to Iris Newgate.

There had not been one item about the woman he had not noticed last night. The delicate sweep of her neck, touched by the silky curls cascading to her shoulders. Her laughter, soft and sweet, rang in his ears. The scent of her lavender bathwater had infused itself into his memory, as real and as fresh as the smoky aroma of the wood fire burning beside him in the grate.

James closed his eyes, letting his head relax against the chair back. The brandy remained untouched on the side table, but a drunken smile rose to his lips at the picture conjured so swiftly in his mind's eye. Iris' gown had fit her like a glove, making James wish he were a glove instead of a man. It would be heavenly to be close enough to the woman to feel her feminine curves against his skin, instead of constantly keeping distance between them for propriety's sake.

When they were walking outside the music hall, James had chanced to glance down and had seen Iris' feet encased in embroidered slippers that were at once both dainty and sensible. She had never stumbled during their stroll, seeming so sure-footed and capable that it had been his desire to touch her rather than her need for stability that had him taking her arm under his. A woman who could not only think on her feet but possessed enough aplomb to require no man's support on those selfsame feet was noteworthy. The manner in which she had conducted herself, chatting and ambling with animation but without any of the typical female wiles on display, had further convinced James that Iris was not a woman to be taken lightly. Not that he needed any extra convincing. He had already decided she was a fine match, hadn't he?

It had been days since his proposal, yet she gave no hint of being ready to offer him an answer. It galled him that he, a man with enough power and influence to expect compliance at every juncture, waited like a schoolboy to be told whether or not he was going to receive the treat he most desired.

He pictured himself sitting on a wall, a child dangling his legs and waiting for someone to come help him down from his perch. It was precisely how he felt, as if his own footing had been sacrificed in his yearning to have hers join his on the precarious path he trod. Frustration mounted when it hit him that Iris Newgate might let him cool his heels on the figurative wall for as long as she liked. He, the man who wielded power as an accountant handles a quill, had handed over control to a woman. How could he have done such a reckless thing? How could he have given Iris his position so freely? And what would she do with the upper hand, assuming she realized she did, in fact, hold all the cards in this match?

"Botheration!" James slapped the arm of his leather chair so hard, his palm stung. "What have I done?"

His eyes shot open when the hinge on the door creaked, announcing he was no longer alone.

The man striding through the door wore dusty riding clothes. The information he carried was obviously such that he had not taken precious moments to clean up before presenting himself.

"I can't say, old man. I have only just arrived and have no idea what you've done." A wide grin split Graham's face as he dropped into a chair on the other side of the hearth. He slapped at his boots with his gloves, sending a cloud of dust and grit into the air. "Why don't you tell me what it is that's got you so peeved? Then maybe I can help you sort things out and perhaps save the arm of your favorite chair as well. So, what do you say? Are you willing to spill your secrets, old man?"

"Don't call me that," James growled. He and Graham had been childhood friends. During their teen years, the nickname had been born of the few months that separated their ages, and somehow it had stuck.

"Whoa, hold on there. I guess you're more disgruntled than I first thought you were." Graham held his hands up in mock surrender. "I didn't mean any harm, old man—oops, that just slid out."

" 'Slid out,' my foot. You can never resist making a jab at my expense, can you?" James shook his head as he watched Graham plow his fingers through his hair. The unruly red mop had been wind-tousled when he entered the room. Now that he had run his hands through it several times, it looked as if a small bonfire sat above Graham's eyebrows.

"You know I can't."

"Well, I wouldn't be so quick to poke fun, Mr. Carrots," he retorted, a chuckle making the words come out in a rush.

Graham raked his fingers through the mess again, making it even worse than it had been. He scowled, echoing the words James had uttered just a short time earlier. "Don't call me that."

"Ah, so the pot doesn't mind calling the kettle a name or two, but the minute the kettle opens its mouth, things are altogether different, are they?" His mood had lightened considerably with Graham's appearance. It had always been that way between them. They were as close as brothers were, and James hoped they always would be. "Turns you puckish, doesn't it, when I call you names?"

" 'Puckish'? I have not heard that word in years. But it is hard to get back into the London lingo after being away so long. I'm working on it, but there are times when I know it's better just to keep my mouth shut and hope no one realizes I'm searching for the right words to say." Going to America had been necessary to their cause, but when Graham had left, no one thought it would mean such a prolonged absence from England. He had not complained when he learned his homecoming would be forestalled, time and again, but then, James had not expected his stalwart companion to kick up a fuss.

"It's good to have you back." James leaned forward, putting a hand on Graham's knee and giving it a quick squeeze. He smiled and then sat back in his seat. "I had no one to spar with while you were off playing with cowboys on the other side of the world."

"It is a wild country, I grant you that much, but there aren't any cowboys in New York City," Graham said. His eyes twinkled mischievously. "Not any that I saw, anyhow. Now, if you do not mind, I would like to get down to brass tacks. Then maybe I'll be able to wash up and hit the hay."

James raised a dubious eyebrow, hardly hiding his amusement. " 'Hit the hay'? You've got to be joking—do those Americans really use such expressions?"

"If you only knew what passes for conversation in New York. Someday soon, when we've got more time and I'm not so bushed—er, when I'm not this spent, we shall have to have a laugh over some of the jargon I picked up while on assignment." Graham placed his gloves on the table beside him and reached inside his coat. He drew out a letter, the dark green sealing wax a giveaway as to the missive's origin. Holding out the letter, Graham said, "But now, I'm afraid, isn't the time. Here is the letter you were hoping to receive. I was privy to the discussion that precipitated it, so I can save you the trouble of reading it by telling you that the plan is uncompromised."

"This baron's murder?"

Graham shook his head. "No bearing whatsoever."

A long sigh of relief escaped James' lungs. His shoulders dropped as the tension left his body. They had all worked too hard, and come too far, to have anything derail their arrangement. The preparations had come with a dear price that had been paid by many, so he was not the only one with much at stake.

"Thank goodness! So there is no hint of an investigation? No chance the law will be on my doorstep before sunrise?"

A crooked grin lit up Graham's face. "You've been awake so long that you didn't see the sunrise, old man. It has been up for an hour, at least. Looks to be another cold, damp day too. I had no idea the weather here was so lousy until I got a taste of New York's crisp fall days. I'll tell you, it really does change a man's focus to see the world from another angle."

"I imagine it does. But the authorities? Shall I expect them?"

"No chance. The letter confirms that; everything has already been taken care of, and no one should bother you about any aspect of the murder. Last night's"—he hesitated, searching for the appropriate words—"*unfortunate event* will just be another in a long line of unfortunate events that have befallen our baronage. Nothing more or less. Nothing, certainly, to concern you. Mostly it will be just another thing to keep tongues wagging over your exploits."

Heaving a deep sigh, James wondered what—if anything—he could have done to prevent his life from becoming this complicated. But he did not see how he could have avoided any of the intricacies of his position. When duty called, he had answered. Until now, the life he led, filled with deception and intrigue, had been satisfactory.

He wondered how he was ever going to be able to successfully add a wife to his long list of obligations.

"Perhaps I should have my head examined," he said. "A doctor might be in order here, someone to investigate my hold on my wits."

Throwing his head back and letting loose a laugh that was sure to wake any servant still slumbering, Graham said, "Now that's the brightest idea you've had in a long, long time, old man. It might be a short visit for the doctor, at that. He might not take any time at all to learn there's too much rattling around in that head of yours for your own good."

Only from Graham would James take such ribbing. He tapped the edge of the still-sealed letter on his knee. "Probably wouldn't take any time at all—you're right. So I will just grow a bit more nefarious, set a few tongues wagging harder in drawing rooms and salons, then? That's the only consequence to us from the murder?"

"That's it. Good for our cause, I would say. A real added bonus, if I do say so myself."

The cause took priority, but James' growing feelings for one very special woman made the bonus feel empty.

"Right," he said. He slid a fingernail beneath the sealing wax and opened the letter. He scanned it swiftly before crumpling the paper in his hand and tossing it into the fire. They watched it catch and then burst into flames. "Did you speak with Anne?"

Graham nodded, stifling a yawn with the back of one hand. "I did."

"And?"

"She agreed to be there. She was not happy about it . . . something about a plan to go to the seaside for the holiday with her sister on their way to Peacock's Roost, but after I stressed the importance of her presence, she gave in. Said she would insist her sister accompany her, and said you would pay for the inconvenience you are causing." Graham paused, his lips twitching with amusement. "So listen, old man, what kind of payment will the good woman demand in exchange? Anything you would care to divulge?"

Waving a dismissive hand, James said, "A quick visit to the jeweler's will be in order, I suppose. Jewels are the best way to soothe a woman's ruffled feathers, don't you think?" A thought, unexpected but completely welcome, swept over him. *The jeweler's!* Why hadn't the idea come to him sooner? Now that it had, he was in a hurry to dispense with the business at hand and to set about putting this newest part of his plan into action.

James rose, and Graham followed suit.

"Anything else?" James asked as they walked toward the doorway. "Anything more I should know, aside from the fact that my reputation has gotten one more dent to it than it had at this time yesterday?"

"No, that seems to be about it." Graham opened the door, and they stepped into the wide, dark-paneled hallway. They went to the front door, then stopped. "I should tell you, though, that there are rumblings among the lowest peers about the lengthening murder-victim list."

"How so?" James kept his hand on the door handle but did not open the door.

"They're saying that they're . . . ah, expendable. And there are a few who are making noises about digging deeper to find some proof and expose the killer."

James shrugged. They could dig until they reached the

other side of the globe; no amount of probing would uncover the truth behind the barons' demise.

He opened the door wide and saw that Graham had been correct. The sun had risen without his knowledge, but while it was light outside, it was definitely not bright. A dull pall, one that matched his mood, brought grayness to the atmosphere. Even the horses plodding on the lane seemed burdened by the day's gloom.

"Let them dig. We both know they cannot touch us." James clapped a hand onto his friend's shoulder. He looked deeply into Graham's eyes and saw that the only thing keeping the other man upright was sheer determination. A bone-weary expression made the usually bright eyes dull. A pang of pity, as well as a measure of regret, hit him hard. Graham had lost a night's sleep because of him. It was not the first he had given up and would not be the last. James softened his tone, giving Graham a gentle push toward the black stallion tied to the hitching post at the end of his walkway. "Go home. Get some sleep. We will devise a plan for the coming days later on this afternoon. For now, you need to rest, and I have a plan of my own to carry out."

Always faithful, Graham stopped halfway between James and his mount. He turned and asked, "Do you require my assistance? I am not so weary I cannot help you."

Graham had never offered anything less than his best effort, whatever the venture. He was giving to a fault, something James appreciated but could not use to his advantage. It would not be fair.

"No, thank you. I am perfectly capable of taking care of this errand."

The leather-bound book brought a satisfying smack when it hit the side table. Iris watched it slide across the polished surface. It came near to toppling off and onto the floor, but it stilled just before tumbling, one thick edge hanging two inches off the wood.

She had thought the soothing passages in the volume of poetry might calm her frayed nerves, but it was obvious they were not up to the task. She had been staring at the pages for hours. The only gift she had received for her effort was the dull headache that hung behind her eyes.

A glance at the ribbon of light peeking in between the folds of the draperies told her that dawn had arrived without her seeing its approach.

Another sleepless night, Iris thought. *How many does that make now?*

Ethel arrived on silent feet, bearing a tray. She set the burden down on a low table in front of where Iris was seated and adjusted the placement of teapot, flatware, china, and plate of scones before straightening. "I thought you might be hungry, miss."

As if on cue, Iris' stomach rumbled. She gasped, covering her middle with one hand. A smile darted across Ethel's face, and Iris admitted with embarrassment, "I suppose I am, at that. Thank you, Ethel. The scones look lovely."

"Cranberry orange, your favorite. Mrs. Perkins thought you might enjoy them this morning, seeing as how last night was so upsetting." Ethel wrapped her arms around herself, looking so upset that Iris was tempted to stand up and hug her. It would not do to be that familiar with the servants, but Iris was tempted.

News might take a full day, or even a few days, to reach drawing rooms, but the servants' network brought current events below stairs much more rapidly. Iris had long ago given up being shocked by the speed with which the staff gleaned information, having realized that her best bet was to appreciate that her grandfather's retainers were forthcoming and shared their news with her.

Still, she had been within touching distance of the dead man and knew next to nothing about the insidious event.

"I will. Please, thank her for me." Iris watched Ethel drop a scoopful of coal onto the fire. It fell onto the grate and was swallowed by the licking flames. Iris shivered at the memory of last night's disastrous turn of events. "And yes, last night was highly upsetting. For everyone, but especially for that unfortunate soul who met his death."

Iris waited, knowing Ethel so well, she knew that if the housekeeper had information to share, it would take but a moment for her to make known her intelligence bulletin.

"Oh, another baron, they are saying! And murdered so foully, to boot." Ethel wrung her hands, her distress apparent.

Iris waited, knowing there was more.

"Stabbed, right through the heart. And so much blood, they're saying." The housekeeper gulped, the sound loud in the still room. For a moment Iris thought she might have to offer Ethel a chair, to keep her from swooning, but she was relieved when Ethel pulled herself together. "And you, being there—oh, it just breaks my heart, it does, knowing anyone could have been standing right beside a murderer all the while. Imagine that, miss! Attending a musicale and ending mixed up with a murderer!"

Imagine that, Iris thought.

Chapter Fifteen

The morning passed in a blur. Iris was glad, because the flurry of activity kept her from her own company—and her own thoughts. Perhaps most important, it saved her from being forced to examine her own heart.

First Catherine arrived, looking so close to swooning that Iris had pulled her down onto the chaise and insisted she put her feet up and rest a while before they talked. When her friend had recovered sufficiently to converse, Iris saw that Catherine had no new news but was focused on reliving the previous evening's events. It was almost as if she thought going over each minute of the musicale might somehow change the course of events.

Iris endured Catherine's prattle for an hour before she begged off, saying she had letters to write and household matters that required her attention. Catherine's leave-taking had been as dramatic as her arrival, with more than one teary embrace on the doorstep. Iris was relieved when the door closed firmly behind the other woman. She leaned against it, pulling in a huge breath of air and holding it in her lungs. Yes, it seemed that

Catherine's theatrical betrothed had made the perfect match. Their life together would be a series of dramas—that much was clear. Iris hoped that some of the couple's adventures would be comedic, if only to lend some relief to the tension they were sure to find in every facet of married life.

Bridget's visit came close on the heels of Catherine's departure. Fortunately for Iris' nerves, the married woman was much less inclined to theatrical gestures.

When they were seated side by side on the soft, cocoonlike cushions on the wide window seat overlooking the side lawn, Bridget wasted no time with idle chitchat. She cast a steely gaze at Iris, smoothed her skirt with her hands, and then said, "I trust you have heard the latest particulars." When Iris sat silently waiting, Bridget went on. "Another baron, Lord Holmes. This time, the baron was less obscure than the others were. In fact, we met him and his wife both, last Season at one of Anne's garden parties. I believe it was the one when the harp player had that unfortunate accident. You can't have forgotten that one, can you?"

Iris fought the urge to giggle. She doubted anyone who had seen the barrel-shaped harpist trip on the hem of her gown and tumble across the back lawn and into the duck pond with a huge splash would forget the scene. The musician's emergence from the water—duck feathers and other detritus stuck wetly to her ensemble—was an unforgettable image.

"No, I haven't forgotten. However, I do not recall the baron. You said he was there with his wife?" She searched her memories of that day for the man but came up empty. "What did she look like? Maybe I can place him by remembering her."

"Tall. Thin. Brown hair and a sharp-featured face. She spent the afternoon looking as if she had spent the morning sucking on a bowlful of lemons. She acted as if she hated harp music, garden parties, and the whole lot of us. I think that's why she's so hard to place; they were on the fringe of society and showed up very rarely at functions." Bridget sighed. In deference to the day, she was clad in a somber navy blue muslin morning dress. It was one of her most severe but was still attractive enough to bring out her classic good looks and dark, flashing eyes. She swept a minuscule bit of lint from her skirt. "Think back, now. If memory serves me, the pair kept to themselves. They stood mainly beneath that large oak tree in the corner of Anne's lawn. Do you recall?"

Clarity struck Iris full force. Of course, she remembered the couple! The baron had given her a head-to-toe open appraisal and a smile too bright and inviting to be shared with a person before the proper introductions had been made. Iris had been chilled by his stare, feeling he could somehow see beneath her petticoats to the bare skin of her legs. His wife had noticed the baron's lascivious stare, and he had earned a sharp elbow in his side for his bad behavior.

"I remember now." Iris shuddered. She could feel, once again, the man's gaze on her as strongly as if she were back on the lawn again. "He had a way about him. . . ."

Bridget nodded. "That's the one. He was famous for being careless where he put his hands. Of course, my husband warned me about the man, and I have always kept enough distance between us that he could not touch me, but it did not keep his smarmy gaze from making me feel ill. We three even discussed the man . . . Why, it had to be at least two Seasons ago, when the first hint of his boorish behavior began to make the rounds. Don't you recall?"

Two Seasons ago Iris had been struggling with losing her grandfather. She barely remembered anything of that time. It was, she was sure, a blessing that she had forgotten most of those difficult days and nights.

"I don't, I'm sorry. I am sure we did discuss the baron, but the conversation seems to have slipped my mind." She took a deep breath, held it, and then let it out slowly. Tension fell from her shoulders, and she lifted a hand and held it, palm up. She shrugged. "Right after Grandfather's passing, remember? It was not one of the highest points in my life, and I have forgotten a lot of what went on during those months."

Patting her hand with a brisk nod, Bridget said, "Oh, right. I am sorry, Iris. I must admit that I try to put those days from my mind whenever I can. They—oh, they simply hurt too much to dwell on."

"Don't apologize. I feel the same way about that time. Anyhow, I do recall the man and his wife, now that you remind me of them. I confess I did not hold him in high regard, but I do regret his death. It hardly put a cheerful end to last night's festivities."

After the woman who discovered the baron's body had been led away, the rest of the crowd had been held inside the music hall for questioning. It had been hours before Iris was ushered into a side office and asked a series of questions about her participation in the event. She had given her statement without deviating from the truth. The only part she had held back were the moments when James had kissed her. Those moments were private, and she was not about to share them with the authorities. Besides, they had no bearing on the baron's murder.

"No," Bridget allowed. "The murder was not the best way to put the night to bed. I do have some news about the baron, though, if you're interested."

"You know I am." Iris took one of Bridget's hands in hers

and squeezed, the same way she had done when they were little girls sharing secrets. "Do tell, Bridget. I cannot stand the suspense of knowing you have details on the crime when I am in the dark."

"Not exactly details on the crime, but something, at least." Bridget paused, intentionally leaving Iris dangling. She had done the same when she was a child, and it had vexed Iris then, but now it made her squeeze the hand she held harder still. "Ouch! You are breaking my fingers! I'll tell—just let go."

"Sorry." Iris grinned as she released Bridget's hand. "You know how I love a mystery, and you look like a cat with a mouthful of feathers."

Bridget leaned so close, their foreheads nearly touched. Then, so quietly that no one could overhear her words, had there been anyone about to do so, she said, "I heard that the baron was neck-deep in debt."

Disappointed, Iris sat back against the pillows. What was the news in that? Everyone knew that each of the dead barons had been drowning under a mountain of personal debt. She had assumed last night's victim to be in the same straits as the others.

"So?" She gave a small shrug. "That's not news, is it? They were all gamblers, weren't they? It seems that aside from all being barons, the other thing the dead men have in common is their passion for gaming. There's no news in that, Bridget."

Looking more like a satisfied cat by the minute, Bridget said, "But that's the most intriguing bit of the puzzle. Lord Holmes did not have a gambler's vice. He—" She cast a furtive glance around the room. They were alone, but she spoke softly anyhow. "He had a vice of an entirely different sort. It is said that Lord Holmes favored the ladies. In particular, he spent his funds in the jewelry shop, purchasing baubles with the hope of winning favor with any number of women."

The times were such that liaisons of that nature were not uncommon. While Iris did not approve of such loose moral values, she was not entirely unaware that there were others who found nothing amiss with keeping a mistress. It was a sad state of affairs, one she hoped never to have intimate knowledge of in her lifetime.

"Many men keep mistresses, Bridget. Their wives look the other way, and all goes on as normal. What makes Lord Holmes any different from so many of his peers?"

Bridget spoke quickly, almost as if she feared losing her nerve if she delayed. "But don't you see? Lord Holmes went broke buying jewels for *married* women! The *on dit* is that he was killed by someone's husband as payment for his misguided gift-giving!"

A sigh of relief flew from Iris' body. She smiled, unable to quell the mad fluttering in her chest.

If Lord Holmes had been killed by an irate husband, that meant James was off the hook. Of course, he had been with her at the musicale, but not the entire time and not nearly long or publically enough to stop the usual tongues from wagging. The baron's reputation might be just what James needed to keep his own name from further tarnish.

By the time the sun was on its descent toward the horizon, Iris was spent. There had been a short respite from the household buzz shortly before lunch. She had used the time to its best advantage and had taken a nap. Her head, so fuzzy-feeling after her long, sleepless night, cleared enough that she spent the hours immediately following her meal catching up on some sadly neglected correspondence.

It was not like her to be remiss in her letter writing, especially since most of those she corresponded with were longtime friends of her grandfather's. When he passed, the quill and parchment became her duty, one Iris generally enjoyed. These last weeks, however, had not lent themselves to furnishing blithe, informative fodder for passing along. However, with the idea that James would not be accused of last night's murder planted firmly in her mind, she felt so at ease that cheerful words spun themselves like silk from the nib of her pen.

The hours had passed peacefully. Iris sealed the final missive with paraffin, pressed Grandfather's signet firmly into the cooling wax, then set the packet aside. There was a tidy heap of sealed letters on one corner of her desk. She sat back in her chair, folded her hands in her lap, and smiled.

It was strange how a bit of good news could cheer someone so completely. This morning she had been certain the day would roll into an extension of last night's horror, bringing more distressing news and nothing by way of explanation for the latest baron's murder. But, as quickly as a breeze clears a cloud from the sky, Bridget's visit had changed everything.

A tap on the door caught her attention. The door opened, and Ethel came into the room. She dipped into a curtsey and then said, "Mr. Clark is here to see you, miss. Shall I send him in?"

"Please do, Ethel. And please bring some tea as well." Iris stood, smoothing her skirt with her hands as she walked to the center of the room.

The solicitor appeared, moving as quickly as his arthritic knees allowed. He bowed, bringing Iris' heart right into her throat. She feared he might topple over, he was so unsteady on his feet, and she took two steps in his direction. She stopped, however, when she saw he was in control, his torso and upper body moving back to their customary position. She did not wish to embarrass the man, so she waited for his gaze to meet hers.

"Mr. Clark. It is so kind of you to call on me this afternoon." Iris extended a hand, indicating the settee and chairs in the center of the room. "I am glad to see you. Won't you have a seat?"

"The pleasure is all mine, Miss Newgate." He waited until she sat, then lowered himself onto the edge of a navy blue side chair. A small leather satchel was clasped in one fist. This he placed upright on the floor, leaning one side against a leg of the table beside his chair. When the satchel had been positioned to his liking, Mr. Clark looked up with a benign smile. Iris watched, fascinated, as the elderly man's face stretched into a wreath of wrinkles.

Ethel's arrival with the tea tray diverted Iris' attention from trying to decipher just what had prompted this visit. Mr. Clark did not typically arrive without a prior appointment. Whatever was on his mind must be more pressing than any of the other matters they had discussed in the past. Whatever could it be?

"May I pour you a cup of tea, sir?"

"Yes, please. That would be lovely. A spot of cream in that, if you don't mind." With a shaky, age-spotted hand, he took the saucer from her and placed it on the table beside him. Iris cringed when the china rattled and prayed he did not spill the hot liquid on himself. She had no thought for the cup and saucer; they could be replaced. But Grandfather's trusted friend and business associate? He was beyond repair or replacement, and she cared that he not come to harm.

Iris held out a small plate of biscuits. She wordlessly pressed the aging man to accept two of the soft oatmeal raisin rounds and smiled when he took her encouragement to heart. They were his favorite biscuits. Mrs. Perkins kept a special tin of the chewy treats for his visits, knowing they were soft enough for his often-painful teeth to handle.

They ate in companionable silence for a few minutes. If she

allowed herself to close her eyes and let her mind wander, Iris knew it would have been effortless to believe there weren't two but three people occupying the room. She felt Grandfather's presence so strongly whenever she was with Mr. Clark that it was never an imposition or bother to entertain him. Letting him leave was often the hardest part of one of his calls.

Finally, the solicitor broke the silence. He placed his empty cup on its saucer and brushed biscuit crumbs from his fingers. Then he cleared his throat.

Iris gazed at him expectantly, knowing her rampant curiosity was about to be assuaged.

"I know you are well aware of the conditions of your late grandfather's will and the terms of the codicil to that document." The old man paused, peering at Iris through his spectacles' thick lenses. He waited until she gave a mute nod before he continued. "Yes, well, as I am quite certain you are of sound mind and body, and as I know for a fact, young woman, that you are one of the brightest ladies I have ever had the pleasure to know personally, I will not bog this conversation down by reiterating the terms and conditions of the aforementioned documents."

"I appreciate that, Mr. Clark." Even at his liveliest, the solicitor had a tendency to drag a conversation to its limits. She was grateful he had deigned to keep their discussion brief and to the point. Now, if the man could just find his point and share it, Iris would be able to relax.

She waited while he cleared his throat again. It crossed her mind to offer another cup of tea to soothe the man's scratchiness, but doing so would further put off the reason for his visit. Thankfully, the second round of throat-clearing seemed to do the trick.

Steepling his fingers, he cast rheumy blue eyes on her and stared for a long moment. Then, each word sounding like a stone dropping into a bucket, he said, "You have a meager length of time remaining with which to secure an offer, my dear. You are aware of this fact, are you not?"

"I am very much aware of it." Butterflies the size of stampeding elephants did a waltz in her stomach. She laid a comforting hand across her midsection.

The action was not missed; Mr. Clark's gaze dropped to where her hand lay, then rose to meet her gaze again. When he spoke again, his voice held more compassion than it had scant seconds earlier.

"I regret I must be the one to remind you of the facts. However, I would be remiss in my duties if I did not bring the point up again." He threaded his fingers together and placed his hands in his lap. The elderly man looked resigned and a little bit grim.

Iris felt his remorse, and she, having been the bearer of less-than-wonderful news herself a time or two in the past, sympathized with his position. She brought lightness to her voice to disguise the sound of the elephants' waltz.

"I completely understand. You and Grandfather worked out this plan for me, and now that he is gone, it falls to you to prod me along on my new path." Iris managed a wavering smile. "I am grateful to you for taking the trouble to come over here and remind me of my obligations. I will adhere, one way or another, to Grandfather's last wishes. I would not wish to . . . disappoint him."

He reached over, placed a cool, thin hand on her wrist, and gave a small squeeze. "Don't ever think you could disappoint your grandfather, Iris. He was never more pleased, or proud, than when he was with you or speaking of you. He loved you with all his heart. That is why it was so important to him that you marry well. He had only your best interests, and happiness, in mind when the terms of his will were drawn up."

"Then why? Why did he match me up with James—oh!—with Lord Whitman?" she asked, correcting herself when her mind failed to filter the question from her heart.

The solicitor sat back, a smug smile playing around the corners of his lips. Iris watched the crinkles at the edges of his eyes deepen as he gave himself over to his amusement.

"Ah, I see you have become more familiar with Lord Whitman." He nodded, satisfaction evident in his voice. "That is good, very good. Your grandfather would be pleased with this turn of events. As for your question, I am not at liberty to say precisely why your grandfather wished this match. I can only comment that I know he did wish it but wanted to leave you open to choose a match on your own if that is what you desired. Barring your giving voice to a wish to accept another's offer, he felt—strongly, I might add—that Lord Whitman would be an ideal candidate for a husband for you. He loved you, Iris. Your grandfather believed that you and Lord Whitman—James— would find your way to love as well."

Her head swam with the details. *Grandfather wanted me to have time to choose my own match. And if I don't, he provided one for me, one he approved of. But what of the gossip flying about Town? Am I to spend the rest of my life dealing with that?*

Mr. Clark, apparently, was not finished offering advice. "There is, you do know, an alternative. One that does not involve becoming betrothed to any man."

She nodded. "Yes. The cottage, with its meager yearly stipend. Quite frankly, Mr. Clark, that option looks fairly promising to me at the moment." His eyebrows shot up, his eyes widened in shock, and his mouth opened, but Iris waved aside his unspoken comment with a nonchalant flutter of her finger-tips. "Really. I tease you not on the point. Truthfully, I have not found any man who entices me to wed." She ignored the voice inside her head that refuted her statement. "And a modest cottage, even with near-abject poverty, seems preferable to an alliance with a . . . Well, we all know what is said around Town about Lord Whitman. Let's not pretend we do not."

Time was too precious to mince words, so she spoke her mind.

The solicitor held up one gnarled finger. "I understand and appreciate your candor, but I must straighten the linens on this messy bed, if you will. First, let make one item crystal clear. If you choose not to become betrothed to any man, the cottage will be yours. It is modest, but it is not unfit for habitation. Your grandfather loved you too dearly to sentence you to conditions that are less than healthy. And two"—he raised a second twisted finger—"the stipend you would receive as part of this option is not large, but it will not make you destitute, either. Again, your grandfather would never have left you impoverished. Never. So please, consider those factors when you mull over your options."

He sat back in his chair but popped forward almost as soon as his spine hit the chair back. His index finger went up again, and this time it jabbed through the air just inches from Iris' nose as he made his final point.

"And, my dear, please give the *on dit* spread about Town only the weight it deserves and not one ounce more. We all know that idle chatter is one of our biggest sports and that not all that is said in polite company is factual." He lifted one white eyebrow and stared into her eyes so seriously, Iris felt he could see right into her soul. "Do you truly believe that your grandfather would propose a match with a man who is as bad as people say he is? Do you sincerely think he would do that to you?"

"I don't," Iris admitted. The point was one she had considered too many times to count. If Grandfather thought James an acceptable husband, then there must be more to the man than she knew. But how to find out the truth? The opportunity had not presented itself thus far, and time to uncover the facts was quickly running out. "But how will I separate—and in twelve days, no less—fact from fiction?"

His chuckle caught her off guard. Far from the raspy, throat-clearing noise he had made earlier, this sound seemed to come from somewhere deep inside him. Somewhere younger and more vibrant than the source of the other sound. Her gaze met his, and, in the watery eyes, she saw a sparkle that made her heart jump. It was a shock to witness the transformation, but there it was, right before her eyes. The aged solicitor took on the countenance of a man half his years and, with a sage nod, gave her the best advice she had received since her grandfather's death.

"Ask your heart, not your head, Iris. Your heart will tell you what you need to know. It will separate rumor from reality. Ask your heart . . . then take its advice."

Chapter Sixteen

Every time I make this tedious journey, I vow I shall not do it again. Then, when the next invitation arrives to visit Elliot House, I forget that I have decided against making this trip again. I simply recall the pleasant memories I have of the place, of parties and people that have been fun and exciting, and I agree." Catherine sighed so deeply, the claret-colored ribbons on the front of her dark gray spencer pulled tightly. "When will I learn to think before accepting an offer?"

So many times these past days Iris had wished she possessed a trait such as the one her dear friend now lamented over owning. Life would be so much less taxing if she could learn to act without thinking as much as she did. It was one of the few personality traits that set the two friends apart. Catherine leaped before she looked, and Iris examined the placement of even a single step before she lifted a foot.

"Oh, your impulsive nature is one of the things I like best about you." The truth came easily and brought a gentle smile to Catherine's face.

"You are too kind."

"I am not speaking out of mere kindness, Catherine. It is true, you are prone to act first and consider second. I, on the other hand, think and think—then think some more—before I decide which direction to pursue. I am too logical by far, too cautious as well. Look at you, already betrothed to a swell of the first stare, while I am lost in limbo. I have options but know not which to pursue." The truth annoyed her, but there was no escaping it.

The start of a headache began to make its presence known in Iris' temples. She removed the glove from her right hand and used her fingertips to massage the area near her right eyebrow. Emma Jean had positioned her hairpins so tightly, they felt like barbs; between the realities of her life and her hairstyle, she suffered more than any woman on the way to a holiday house party should. "If only I could be more like you and decide one way or the other, I believe I would be so much more content."

"Cats are 'content.' They have bowls of cream and warm chairs to lounge on, hands to stroke them, and not a care in the world to occupy their minds."

Iris attempted to follow the thread of her companion's thinking. It was not an easy matter to get inside Catherine's head, but, since she had had a lifetime of practice, Iris understood the implication. She smiled, grateful to be on the upper end of one of Catherine's comparisons.

"And I am not a cat. That is your point, isn't it?"

"Precisely." Catherine folded her hands in her lap and looked at Iris with the eye of a teacher on a star pupil. Obviously there was more to the comparison, but, try as she might, Iris did not make the connection, thus giving Catherine a second opportunity to heave a long, ribbon-tightening sigh. "Cats have no opinions. They take no part in making decisions that will affect any aspect of their lives. They are entirely dependent on others for everything—entertainment, warmth, food, love. They cannot think for themselves, not one whit."

"How do you know that is the case? Have you ever conversed with a cat or been told from the cat's own whiskers that it is without its own thoughts?" Teasing Catherine now proved as much fun as it had been when they were children. Iris' threatening headache abated as she watched her friend squirm to come up with a reasonable response.

"That's not the point!" Catherine exclaimed. Then she laughed, seeing the conversation for what it was. "And you know it too. All I am saying is that you have a head on your shoulders that is of greater use than sheer decoration or to provide a spot upon which Emma Jean may style your hair. Believe me, if I were given the choice between a contemplative nature and a reckless one, I would choose contemplation any day. It is much less likely to cause anyone to raise a stir. In addition—you know this is true—you have hardly ever found yourself to be in the suds. I, on the other hand, am there too often by far."

Laughter bubbled up inside Iris, filling her with lightness of the sort she had not felt in days. Leave it to Catherine to pull her out of her mawkish misery. How could anyone be slack-jawed when face-to-face with a temperament like Catherine's?

She made no attempt to point out the holes in Catherine's cat theory. While she appreciated the light tone of her dear friend's comparison, it was not entirely true that cats could not think or fend for themselves. Feral cats did a fine job of finding food and shelter, and all without human intervention. Still, she appreciated the caring behind Catherine's teasing, so she let the matter drop uncorrected.

Shaking her head fondly, she lost any thought of being overwhelmed by her state of affairs. She shrugged. "Oh, I have been in my own share of trouble, and frequently enough. You, and Bridget as well, know that to be the case."

"Of course, we've all been in a scrape or two," Catherine allowed. She glanced out the window at the endless stream of leafless trees that passed for scenery at this bleak point in the year. Bringing her gaze back to Iris', she said softly, "But Bridget and I both agree that you will find a way to get yourself out of this new basket of mischief. We know you will, with all your wit and wisdom, figure out the best course of action."

Iris wished she were as sure as everyone else seemed to be. From Mr. Clark's advice to follow her heart to this new bit of friendly advice to let her mind dictate her course, there seemed no end to the paths open before her. *How to choose?* Iris thought as her head began to throb again, more persistently this time.

The carriage wheels hit a particularly deep rut, sending the women flying off their seats. Catherine's hair hit the upholstered roof, while Iris was merely jostled.

"Ooh, that hurt!" Catherine wound her fingertips into her crown of braided hair and massaged her scalp, a scowl marring her pretty features. "Remind me next time an invitation to Elliot House arrives that I am not going to make the trip. I cannot do this again; it is too tedious by far, and, honestly, if you had not agreed to make the trip with me, I would be so lonesome, I would be in tears by now."

A second carriage carrying their trunks—as well as Emma Jean and Catherine's maid, Christy—rode behind them. It was a serviceable vehicle but not as road-worthy as the one they occupied. Iris scooted across her seat to the window. She stuck her head out and peered behind them. What she saw brought a cry to her lips.

"Jackson! Stop the carriage!"

Catherine had taken to her bed the moment they reached their rooms. Claiming that the horror of the carriage crash had brought on a case of the vapors, she had allowed Christy to draw her bath and tuck her in. Hours later, there was still no sound coming from the room adjoining Iris', leaving Iris to assume that her friend was still indisposed.

Being on her own suited her purposes just as well as having company would have done. Either way, she was still at sixes and sevens, torn in so many directions, she could hardly think. By the time they reached their destination tomorrow afternoon, she would be down to having only nine days left before she would have to admit she had not been able to decide her own fate.

That was what nagged her the most, that she could not make a decision.

Iris rubbed her forehead tiredly, easing the worry lines with her fingers.

Their rooms were on the second floor of the inn and faced the road. Horses' hoofbeats and the rumbling of carriage wheels had been filling the air for hours, but until a few minutes ago, there had not been a commotion like the one that reached her ears now.

Iris darted to the window, pushing aside the curtain and peering out into the late-afternoon gloom. The fashionable carriage parked below was familiar to her. She had seen it before . . . but where? When the door swung wide and the steps were lowered into place, the feeling that she knew the owner of the rig grew more insistent. The moment she saw who stepped from the carriage, her heart soared.

She grabbed the silver bell on the table beside her bed and rang it, hard.

Emma Jean entered from the dressing room, which also served as her accommodations for their stay. She dropped to a curtsey. "Yes, miss?"

Iris reached for a sheet of paper from the desk and scrawled a quick note. A fast dusting of powder set the ink well enough that the note could be folded. She handed the folded square to her maid. "Lady Hargrove-Smythe has just arrived. Her carriage is still in the front courtyard. Please have this delivered to her, and wait for an answer."

"Certainly, miss."

As Iris watched the door close behind the servant, she could not help but wonder what had brought Anne so far from London. It was out of character for her to venture out so soon after her Fall Fete. Typically, she retired to her country home for the holiday season. In fact, Iris had never known Anne to attend any Christmas or New Year's event. It was more her style to hibernate through the winter and emerge refreshed and ready for spring's festivities.

Something had enticed Anne to stray from her schedule. But what? Or who?

Lady Hargrove-Smythe was gracious enough to invite Iris to tea, so there was an opportunity to ask her questions in person.

When tea had been poured and she had nibbled the edge of a watercress sandwich, Iris allowed herself to broach an inquiry. She hoped she did not seem nosy but could not keep herself from asking that which burned her tongue, she was so keen to have an answer.

"Whatever brings you out this far from London, Anne? I do not mean to stick my nose where it does not belong, but I have never known you to be out and about this far past the end of the Season." Iris smiled apologetically, holding her hands wide and open. She shrugged, claiming her curious nature as her own. What else could she do? "You are usually ensconced in your lovely country estate—Peacock's Roost, I think it's called, isn't it?"

Peacock's Roost lay two hours north of London, in an area where rolling hills and thick forests encouraged wild peacocks to seek their homes. It was said that Anne's estate boasted hundreds of the birds, although Iris assumed that number to be far in excess of the actual count. After all, who would encourage so many birds to roost—and do other things as well—on their lawns? It did not seem sensible in the least.

"Peacock's Roost. Yes, that is the spot. And really, Iris, you must visit me there sometime. Please, say you will." Anne made it impossible to refuse, so Iris nodded. "Good. It is settled, then. We will find a time for you to visit, and that will be that. Then you shall get to see some of my beloved creatures up close. Oh, they are so lovely. . . ."

A suspicion swept over Iris, one she had no reason to feel, but it niggled at her anyhow. Anne's effusive invitation, as well as her starry-eyed rendering of the birds at her estate, struck a false note. Iris did not believe the other woman was embroidering or dissembling about anything connected with her cherished country home; however, she felt the hollow ring in Anne's words. They seemed designed to lure Iris from her original question. She refused to be dissuaded.

"They must be gorgeous. I shall look forward to seeing them and your home as well. We shall find a suitable time and enjoy a pleasant visit." Iris swept the social niceties before the crux of her inquiry. "But, as I was saying, most—if not all—years at this time you are already snugged in for the winter months at Peacock's Roost. It seems odd to see you so far afield and on such a dismal day. What brings you out this way, Anne? Nothing serious, I hope."

Anne's eyebrows rose, and her nose twitched as if she found the idea accompanied by a repellent odor. She shook her head. "No, nothing serious. As you well know, I am not of a solemn nature, my dear." She grinned, as if to punctuate her point. "No, my journey is by way of repaying an old debt, you could say. I was encouraged to attend the holiday festivities at Elliot House. I initially declined, saying that I had already arranged to return to Peacock's Roost, but . . ." She lifted her shoulders and then let them fall. A small grin illustrated her predicament. "But what could I do? Truly, I could not refuse the request, not when it came from someone who has done me a number of turns in the past."

Iris bit her lower lip. Any number of possible faces popped into her mind; it was almost impossible to know exactly who had been bold enough—and had so much influence—to put Anne on the spot.

"I understand." Iris hoped her words hid her inquisitive temperament. It was all she could do not to jump out of her seat and demand to know the identity of the person who had coaxed the cream of society to do his bidding. The question of gender did not once cross Iris' mind; she was certain a man was responsible for Anne's journey. Her lip found its way back to its position between her teeth, and she worried it briefly before gathering her thoughts. "It is quite . . . um, quite surprising, isn't it, the number of debts we accrue in a lifetime? Debts, both financial and social, that need to be repaid by some means."

Anne raised an eyebrow. She was shrewd and used to dealing with sticky social situations. Iris saw that her chatter did not disguise her curiosity.

"Ah, yes. Debts. Allow me to speak candidly, Iris. I suspect you are in quite deep—a result, of course, of your grandfather's debts."

Instinctively Iris straightened her spine and squared her shoulders. She frowned, annoyed by the inference. "Certainly not! My grandfather did not leave me in dire straits at all. When he passed, all of his accounts were quite up to date, thank you. There was nothing at all for me to concern myself with." A new thought occurred to her, and the furrows in her forehead deepened. "And I'll have you know that anyone who says otherwise is selling a bag of moonbeams. Upon my word, my grandfather left no debts behind, and anyone who disputes that will have to deal with me."

Anne leaned forward and placed a gentle hand on Iris' arm. Her tone was conciliatory and soothing. "I meant no disrespect, my friend. No harm, either. No one has been spreading Banbury tales about your grandfather or his finances. No, I just surmised that you might be somewhat purse-pinched, now that you are alone. That is all, I promise."

Somewhat mollified, Iris relaxed her posture a touch. She had jumped to conclusions, letting herself be drawn into a defensive pose. It was regrettable. She softened, saying, "There is more to life than wealth, Anne. Much more. Grandfather did not leave me wealthy, but I am more than capable of taking good care of myself. I just do not want anyone to think that I am in need of funds. As I said, I do sincerely believe that wealth is not the highest priority in life. At least, it is not in mine."

A smile played across Anne's face. She looked satisfied. "I am glad to hear it. In addition, just to show you that there are no hard feelings between us, and to let you see we are still as close as ever, I will answer the question that you are so eager to ask. But first, I have one of my own. Have you procured a second carriage to replace the one that crashed this afternoon?"

Emma Jean must have discussed their calamity with Anne's maid. It was the most logical explanation for the knowledge becoming public.

"No, we haven't." The carriage carrying their things had broken an axle and needed repairs that would take more time than either Catherine or Iris were willing to wait. They had tried, without success, to hire a carriage. "We could not, so we shall all pile into the carriage Catherine and I rode in and hope for the best."

"You shall do no such thing." Anne smiled, easing the harshness of her words. "I always have an empty carriage follow along, in case of just such an emergency. It is better to be prepared than not, I always say. Therefore, since I have no use for the additional carriage and you so obviously do, you will use the spare. It will make the remainder of the journey more pleasant, by far, than it would be if you were forced to sit atop your baggage and hold your maid's hand."

Iris was momentarily stunned into silence by the other woman's generosity. Then she pulled her into an impulsive, albeit brief, hug. "Thank you! I am more appreciative of your kindness than I can say. Honestly, I was not sure how we would manage to fit so much into one carriage, but I thought that if need be we could leave my trunk behind and send for it later."

"Oh, that is a dreadful idea," Anne said, laughing. "You do not want to arrive at a house party with only one traveling dress in your entire wardrobe. It would cause quite a stir, your wearing the same dress to every occasion."

It would indeed display her to a poor advantage, but what were her options? Until Anne's gracious offer, there had been none that Iris could see.

"You are right about that. It would set tongues wagging, wouldn't it? But I supposed it would only be for one night, or perhaps a night and half a day, until my trunk could be retrieved."

Anne cast an incredulous gaze Iris' way. "One night? Even that would be far too long to be seen wearing a single dress, my dear! No, this will work out better for everyone and cause no undue stress, so you do not need to thank me. Now, go on. I am not one to make an offer and then renege on that offer."

"Pardon?"

"You have been dying to ask who had called in a favor and persuaded me to journey so far, haven't you?"

Iris shrugged. She had been found out. Why deny it?

"Yes, I did." She plunged ahead. The cat was already out of its bag; she might as well solve the mystery. "To whom did you owe a debt so large that you agreed to spend the Christmas holiday at Elliot House?"

A wide smile lit Anne's face. With a singsong note in her voice, she replied, "James Whitman, of course."

Chapter Seventeen

Iris and Catherine arrived at Elliot House without any fanfare. Anne's spare carriage, laden with their servants and baggage, rolled around to the back of the redbrick mansion while Jackson reined in their carriage before the wide front walkway.

A butler immediately opened the door, dispatching two footmen who helped Iris and Catherine disembark. They were ushered into the entrance hallway.

The butler received them with a polite nod of his gray-capped head.

"Welcome to Elliot House. Lord and Lady Elliot and their guests are out riding at the present. They will be back in time for tea. Rooms have been readied for your arrival. Miss Thane will escort you upstairs." He nodded again and, with a sweeping hand, deposited them directly into the care of the waiting Miss Thane.

They followed her up the thickly carpeted staircase on silent feet, quietly noting the unchanged, always polished and presentable appearance of the interior of the mansion. Both women had visited the estate before. It was one of the premier country manses that were predictably accommodating and reassuringly consistent whenever one arrived.

Their rooms were to the right of the stair landing and down a long, straight hallway. The walls were lined with gilt-framed paintings of generations of Elliots. The costumes and faces changed over time, but the aristocratic glint in every Elliot's eye tied the family portraits together. In addition, the presence of a horse in every picture bound them tightly.

The Elliots were well-known purveyors of fine horseflesh. Their stables were just as immaculate and reliable as the house in which the family resided. It was no surprise to find the party on a morning ride. Morning rides would be, unless the weather proved particularly inclement, *de rigueur* here at Elliot House. They had been in the past, and tradition like that was not likely to be broken.

Iris and Catherine had rooms directly across the hallway from each other. They went their separate ways at their doors, promising to catch up in an hour or so. That was all the time either of them needed to refresh themselves and change from their traveling clothes to morning frocks.

Iris had scarcely removed her gloves and glanced about the cheerful blue-and-yellow room she had been given when there was a harsh knock on the door. *Who can that be? Emma Jean would never rap so briskly.*

She went to the door and pulled it wide rather than calling out for the person on the other side to enter. She did not know who would be waiting. A number of possibilities went through her mind, but none prepared her for what she found.

Catherine, still clad in her spencer and bonnet, raised her closed, gloved fist the moment the door swung open. There was a crumpled sheet of paper in her hand. The familiar navy blue sealing wax staining the front of her glove gave a hint to the origin of what could only be a letter of some sort from Catherine's betrothed, Ethan Harding.

Iris pulled Catherine inside and closed the door behind her. Her hand stayed on Catherine's wrist, which was trembling so hard, Iris could feel the vibrations all the way into her own shoulders.

"What is it?" she asked.

She knew it could only be terrible news. What else would bring Catherine so clearly to a state of near collapse? Images of death—Ethan's own or even that of one of Catherine's parents—chilled Iris as they filled her mind. Catherine's younger sister, Caroline, was everyone's darling. If something had happened to the child, Catherine would never recover. Her elder sister, married to an earl shortly before Grandfather's death, was expecting her firstborn. Perhaps some mishap had befallen her. Worse yet, maybe she had lost the babe.

Oh, pray it is not so. No more loss; we have scarcely recovered from Grandfather's passing, Iris thought, her heart in her throat.

When Catherine stared mutely at her, tears sliding down her blotchy cheeks, her nose running onto her upper lip, Iris gave her a gentle shake. "Catherine! What is it? What has happened?"

A wail escaped Catherine's lips, a jumble of words mixed in with her sobs. It took a second to decipher what she was saying, but when she did, Iris wanted to shake her friend harder still.

Theatrics over an unfortunate inconvenience! It was absurd and childish—and completely in keeping with Catherine's character. Iris wished Bridget were here to deal with this. She had more patience by far and could soothe Catherine better than almost anyone else could.

"He's not coming. . . ." Catherine's words were borne on an anguished cry.

For the tiniest second Iris was abashed at her own lack of compassion. Then she remembered that these histrionics were over a missed social engagement, and she stiffened her lip.

Catherine wailed, "Ethan—is—delayed!" Each word that burst from her was punctuated by a gasp.

Catherine looked ready to be ill, so Iris led her to a chair and pushed her head down between her knees. She retrieved her own lace-edged hanky from her skirt pocket and pressed it into Catherine's hand, taking the smashed letter as she did so. She scanned the note, which was blessedly short and to the point.

"Ethan's been delayed." The fact hardly warranted so many tears.

Iris knelt beside her friend and dropped the note to the floor. She helped Catherine straighten, relieved when she saw there was more color behind the red splotches on Catherine's cheeks. She no longer looked in danger of swooning, so Iris untied the ribbons beneath Catherine's chin. The bonnet came off without a fuss. Then, as if she were undressing a child, Iris pulled off the gloves and untied the ribbons on the front of Catherine's spencer.

A loud, wet-sounding blow into the hanky followed. Catherine's eyes were red-rimmed when her gaze finally met Iris' own.

"I thought he would be here for Christmas. I thought we would begin planning the wedding." Catherine gulped, a small hiccup following closely on the end of her words.

"It is unfortunate that Ethan has been delayed. But isn't absence supposed to make hearts grow fonder? And won't the reunion be sweeter for having been put off?"

Her attempt at restoring Catherine's good humor was met with a cold stare.

"You cannot understand how I feel. You cannot know what it is to love a man so deeply that every thought you own, every breath you take, is dedicated to him. Taken for him, and about him . . . and with the hope that you will be near him again sooner rather than later." She stood, her fists clenched at her sides. As Iris rose, she saw that handfuls of her traveling dress were wadded in Catherine's hands.

Catherine's words cut Iris to the bone. She was stunned and did not know what to say. She felt raw, exposed, and even somewhat betrayed. How dare Catherine accuse her of not knowing how it felt to be in love?

The realization hit her as hard as a fist. She *did* know how it felt to be in love. She knew it with every fiber of her being, didn't she? Whether she was willing to openly admit it or not, her heart had lost its battle with her sensible mind, and she was in love. Deeply in love. Oh, yes, her traitorous heart had given itself away, and there was no rescinding it.

Iris came slowly to her senses. Any attachment of her heart was hers and hers alone, not something to be quarreled over with one of her supposed best friends. Catherine was hurt, true, and angry, but there was no need for her to spread those emotions to Iris. And that was, unfortunately, precisely what she had done with her outburst.

Striving to keep her own soreness from her voice, Iris said, "I did not think that I needed to understand anything more than that you are in pain, and I wished to comfort you." She paused, searching for words that would not heap more ill feelings onto the situation. "I can only say that if it is, as you insist, true love that drives you to such distraction, then I . . . I surely do not want any part of it. If loving someone can bring you to say such hurtful things, I wish to remain as I am."

Unable to contain her own muddled emotions much longer,

Iris crossed the room, opened the door, and held it wide. She did not meet Catherine's eyes when she said as gently as she could, "Now, if you will excuse me, I would like to rest a while before the riding party returns."

Two hours later, Iris and Anne were taking a turn around the library when Catherine entered the room. Iris waited, wondering if Catherine would join them, but she did not. Instead, she selected a volume from one of the shelves and then departed the room with it.

"Is Catherine feeling unwell? She looks rather Friday-faced, don't you think?" Anne asked. She was not the type to miss any detail, so it did not surprise Iris that she picked up on the somber face that had not so much as glanced their way.

Diplomacy seemed the best tactic. Even though she had been wronged, it would be small-minded to deal a blow to Catherine's character. Iris shrugged, avoiding Anne's gaze by keeping hers turned to the bookshelves as they strolled past them.

"I suppose anyone can have the occasional fit of the blue-devils. It is not unusual to be sad or weary after such a long trip. Many are afflicted thus, and Catherine is no exception." Their arms were linked, so Iris put a reassuring hand on Anne's shoulder. "Do not worry about her. I have known Catherine almost all my life. She has a naturally sunny disposition; these small downturns generally pass very quickly. I wouldn't be surprised if she is kicking up a lark again by dinnertime."

"I hope you're right. I have heard rumblings of her betrothed, Ethan Harding, staying away longer than first anticipated. I would hate to think that is what brings her to such despair."

It was hard to maintain a bland expression. Catherine had just learned of Ethan's plans; how was it that Anne's information was almost speedier than the note that lay wadded in the fireplace grate in Iris' room?

"I have heard that romance can take a soul to the pinnacle of ecstasy, as well as the depths of despair." Iris paused, choosing her next words with care. She was annoyed with Catherine but refused to reveal any of her secrets. Any slip of the tongue might be taken as a sign of something more than it was meant to be by someone as intuitive as Anne was. "I would not venture a guess as to the effect a prolonged separation might have on a kindhearted soul."

They reached the glass doors that faced the courtyard and stood before them, looking out. Leafless trees and brown, dying grass surrounded the paving stones. The scene was dismal and oppressive, but they were separated by glass, so somehow it was more like gazing at a painting than a slice of life.

"And what about your heart, Iris? Your soul?" Anne leaned close, her stance inviting confidences. "Tell me . . . Has your heart been claimed yet, my dear? You can confide in me; we are old friends, aren't we? After all, you have agreed to stay with me at Peacock's Roost. I do not, I guarantee you, invite just anyone to my special hideaway."

There was something quite exhilarating about the invitation to confide. Iris was sorely tempted, but in the end she could not divulge the secrets of her heart. It seemed wrong—when she had barely acknowledged them herself—to share them with anyone else.

She shook her head, denying what she truly felt. The deception was not designed to hurt anyone but, rather, to protect her own heart. Surely, that could not be deceitful.

"I am delighted to be counted among the fortunate invited to visit Peacock's Roost," Iris murmured. She cast a grateful glance toward her companion. "I look forward to—"

Loud footsteps echoed through the hall outside the library. Then the door was pushed wide, and jovial voices filled the air. Iris and Anne turned to the sounds, their shoulders bumping together in their rush to see who had joined them.

"James! I wondered when you would arrive!" Anne crossed the room with her arms open wide in greeting. "I have waited all day to hear your voice. And you are not alone. Why, you have both arrived together—how exciting! Iris, do come over and greet James. And you do know his companion, don't you?"

Iris felt rooted to the parquet flooring as the three figures near the door turned their attention her way. The elation that lifted her heart when she heard James' familiar voice was squashed by the amused grin flitting across the face of the red-haired man standing beside him.

She would have loved to run and hide, but that was out of the question, so she squared her shoulders and gave a polite, if stilted, smile. She swallowed convulsively, hoping to wet the tongue that felt glued to the roof of her mouth. Fortunately, she was spared the embarrassment of speaking.

Turning his attention to Anne, James' red-haired companion said, "I am afraid that I have not been properly introduced to your companion, Anne. It would please me greatly if you would do the honors."

"Oh, I am so sorry, Graham. I thought you knew each other. My mistake!"

Chapter Eighteen

Dinner was a strained affair for Iris, but for everyone else seated at the long dining table it seemed like a party. The Elliots, and those who had ridden with them, were in high spirits. Countless tales of past riding and hunting adventures kept the conversation flowing. There was no need to contribute more than an occasional nod or smile or to murmur, "How interesting!" from time to time, which suited Iris' mood just fine.

Seated between Lord Handley, a lesser earl whose sole concentration was on the meal before him, and Lord Yarrow, a man who was fully engaged in reliving his last foxhunt with another avid huntsman seated across from them, Iris toyed with the food on her plate. Under different circumstances she would have enjoyed the sumptuous courses, but tonight everything tasted the same. Bland, dull, and each forkful on the verge of catching in her throat.

Catherine sat beside the hunter who conversed with Lord Yarrow. She made several attempts to catch Iris' eye, but Iris did not allow her to do so. There were enough mixed feelings cluttering her mind; the last thing she needed was to have Catherine add even more to her inner turmoil.

Why had she agreed to attend this holiday party? Hadn't it been enough that her legal time piece was winding down without bringing her situation out in public? She shuddered just thinking about her position.

"I say, are you chilled?" Looking up from his half-eaten quail, Lord Handley cast a solicitous gaze her way. It was the first time he had asked a personal question of her. "Would you like me to have a shawl brought for your shoulders? I can do that, you know." He placed his fork on the edge of his plate and motioned for a servant.

Iris stilled him with a polite smile. She was grateful, but she was warm enough without having to drape a shawl over her. "No, thank you. That will not be necessary. I am fine. Really, I am fine."

He looked doubtful. "If you are sure . . ."

"I am. Thank you just the same." She waved the servant away and then turned her attention back to her plate. Searching for some topic of conversation that was neither riding related nor personal, she stuck a bit of meat into her mouth and chewed as slowly as she could, thinking the action would give her extra time to ponder.

"Happens to me all the time," the man beside her said. He mimed a shiver, then smiled. "I think it must be someone walking across my grave, or where my grave will be eventually. Rather morose thought, actually, isn't it?"

Iris shot him a small smile, grateful for his attempt at glossing over the incident. "Just a bit," she admitted. "But a good explanation, nonetheless."

That seemed to satisfy him. With a nod, he resumed

eating his meal. Once again Iris was on her own and pleased to be so.

It would be horribly impolite to excuse herself before dinner was over. Then it would seem rude if she was to leave before the women retired to the drawing room for polite female conversation. But when the men joined the women for card games, conversation, and dancing, it might be acceptable if she pleaded having a headache and left the group to retire early.

Yes, that is precisely what I shall do, Iris thought with a glimmer of relief. *That way I will be spared the prospect of being drawn into speaking with anyone.*

The only solution to tonight's sticky situation was to make it impossible for anyone to discover any of the secrets she struggled to conceal: her acquaintance with Graham, the spat with Catherine, or, most important, the betrayal her heart had dealt her. By tomorrow, she would surely have devised a better course of action. For tonight, seeking solitude as quickly as possible seemed best.

As soon as the last course had been consumed and the crowd began to move into other parts of the enormous house, Iris saw her opportunity for escape. She headed with the other women down a long hallway in the direction of the drawing room, but when the hallway reached a juncture, she turned to the right rather than the left. While the other women moved along in a cacophony of chatter and rustling skirts, she walked on silent feet, unnoticed and not yet missed, in search of someplace quiet.

Harriet Elliot, their hostess, kept a small sitting room for intimate visits. Iris had had the pleasure of sitting there on many occasions, and now she hoped against hope that the room was unoccupied. She did not think Harriet would mind her using the space. It was the ideal spot for quiet contemplation, a true escape from the bustle of activity that filled the rest of the mansion.

James watched Iris leave the dining room with the other women. He saw the way she lagged behind. His gut clenched, and for one hopeful moment he thought she might turn back. Glance his way. Meet his gaze and see the burning question in his eyes. But, alas, she kept walking.

Her gown swirled delicately around her ankles, making it look as if she floated on air. He remembered how she had felt pressed against him, the soft silkiness of her clothing rustling between them as he tasted her sweet lips.

It stuck in his throat that she had not looked up at him all evening. Many times he had attempted to catch her eye, but she was almost stubborn in her refusal to lift her head in his direction.

While it was well known that there were women who feigned disinterest in order to keep an admirer hanging on, he could not believe Iris was that shallow. So if she wasn't avoiding him with the intent of furthering his desire, could it be that her posture was an attempt to dissuade him from winning her affections?

He raked a hand through his hair, his fingernails scratching his scalp. The tingling shots of pain were welcome, taking some of the sting from the knife that pierced his heart.

Perhaps he had overestimated his appeal. When they had kissed in the moonlight, he thought she returned his favor. Her acceptance to wed him had seemed a certainty, so much so that he had gone to the jeweler the very next afternoon.

Botheration! Could he have read her signals so wrong? Had he become so immersed in deceit, deception, and foolhardy political wrangling that he was too jaded to see what was clearly right before his eyes?

Thank goodness, Iris thought as she entered the deserted sitting room. She had the place to herself. A fire burned low in the grate, giving off sufficient warmth that the room was cozy. Shadows danced on the walls from the glow the flames sent out, bringing the space alive even though she was alone. The room matched her contemplative frame of mind.

Iris took a seat beside one of the windows, on a low settee that afforded a clear view of the night sky through the wide, un-covered glass panes. As if drawn by an invisible string, her gaze shifted upward. The sky was cloudless and dark, just right for stargazing.

There was only one constellation she searched for. It had been so apparent when they stood on the patio at Vauxhall; now the stars twinkled in a tangle. How would she find what had once been obvious but was now hidden?

"Iris?"

Her head swung around at the sound of Catherine's voice. She had not heard the door open, she was so wholly intent upon searching the stars. Catherine stood inside the door, her hands clasped in front of her and an all too familiar expres-sion on her face. Iris had seen the look many times.

Catherine had realized the part she had played in the after-noon's skirmish.

Iris rose, going quickly to stand near her friend. It was not difficult to forgive a friend, especially when she knew Cather-ine's heart to be good. Everyone stumbled now and then; what nature of friendship would they share if either was unwilling to overlook the other's faults and foibles?

"I hope you don't mind my following you. I—I had to

speak with you." A sheen of unshed tears glittered in Catherine's eyes. She looked pleadingly at Iris. "I have to apologize. I said things today I never should have said, let alone thought. I—I am not sure what came over me, but I am truly sorry. Can you . . . Oh, Iris, can you ever forgive me?"

It pained her to see Catherine so close to bursting into tears. No thought was needed; Iris put her hands out and, crossing the space between them, pulled her companion into a close hug.

"Of course I forgive you, Catherine. No harm has been done to our friendship, I assure you." She patted Catherine the way a mother would, hoping to calm the shoulders that shook against her own. "There, there. All is well between us. Stop shaking so—you are giving me quite a fright."

They drew apart. Now that they were face-to-face, Iris saw that the tears swimming in Catherine's eyes were not the first she had shed recently. So, she had been crying all afternoon. It was no great leap to see that something besides Ethan's letter and their row was giving Catherine fits.

"What's wrong? I know it must be more than your not spending the holiday with Ethan. And our silly spat cannot have given you such a hangdog expression. Come now, tell me what has you at sixes and sevens."

Words fell from Catherine's mouth in a mad rush. The dam had burst, and with it all of her fears found a voice. "I have felt for some time that we are growing apart—Ethan and I. His letters are vague and no longer as filled with sentiment as they once were. They arrive less frequently and are not as lengthy. Oh, what can I say? I was not entirely shocked by the message that awaited my arrival. Not shocked, but upset nonetheless."

"Any woman would be upset by the disappointment. It seems only natural." Iris placed a reassuring hand on Catherine's shoulder. "You expected him to catch you up and were unhappy when you learned he would not do so. No one would have thought you would react any differently."

Catherine's gaze dropped to the patterned rug beneath their feet. She did not meet Iris' eyes for several moments, and Iris suspected she knew the reason.

It had been clear for some months that Catherine was more enamored of the idea of Ethan than with the true-life reality of their arrangement. She had played at feeling excitement, anticipation, and an assortment of other equally suitable emotions, but, for those who knew her best, the show was not heartfelt enough to fool them.

Catherine's gaze rose. Iris saw that her notion was correct.

"You do not love him, do you?"

There was no faltering in the head shake. "No. I don't."

"Does Ethan know?"

"I believe he does," Catherine admitted, the words borne on a sigh. "Our feelings are mutual, I think. No, I know we are in accord on this point. I wanted to be in love with him—truly, I did—but I must face facts. I am not, and he is not . . . We are not. This delay in clearing the matter up, this holiday absence from the festivities is what pushed me over the edge. I could not fathom that he would not want to see me, would not desire to set things straight between us, when all I want to do is . . ." She closed her eyes and shook her head, looking thoroughly overwhelmed by it all.

A gentle fingertip pushed Catherine's chin higher. Iris met her gaze and smiled. "Do not despair so. It seems that you and Ethan have already come to a parting of the ways, romantically speaking. You both know it. It is a mere formality before you end your betrothal. Why let it vex you so? It seems better to realize you are not suited for each other now than to wed and find out later."

"You make a valid point," Catherine agreed. A resigned smile chased some of the sadness from her features. "And since we are both aware of it, there seems no need to spoil the holidays by moping, does there?"

"No, there doesn't."

One deep, shuddering breath, and then Catherine cheered somewhat. "Well, now that that is settled, all is well with the world, I would say. Or as well as it is likely to be for the time being. I am grateful for your understanding—and for your friendship, Iris. Whatever would I do without you?"

They hugged as tightly as sisters might. Iris prayed that they never would have to know what it was like to be separated or unable to rely upon each other.

"I am going back to the party." Catherine cocked her head, staring intently into Iris' eyes. "You are planning to join us, aren't you?"

"In a while, perhaps."

Catherine looked skeptical over taking her leave, so Iris waved an encouraging hand toward the door.

"Go on, Catherine. It is all right. I am fine. I just need . . . oh, I do not know. I suppose I just need some time to sit and think, in quiet. I shall see you after a bit. Go on . . . Please, feel free to go back to the others."

She watched Catherine take a few steps toward the door. Then she stopped and turned, an eyebrow raised and a confused look on her face.

"If you're sure . . ."

"I am," Iris said with a nod. "Quite sure."

Chapter Nineteen

Flickering points of starlight danced beyond the wide window-panes, high in the black sky, pulling Iris deep beneath their magical spell. The fire had burned so low, it was barely a glow in the grate. After Catherine's footsteps had faded and she was sure she was on her own, Iris had doused the candles in the cozy room.

Now, reclining on the crushed velvet settee beside the window, she was more relaxed than she had been in days. Months, perhaps. This time alone had done wonders for her soul and had given her the solace to grasp the direction she searched to find.

She knew, finally, what she was going to do. There were no more judgments to be made regarding betrothals, men, or codicils. The decision was abundantly clear.

Iris chose the small cottage and humble stipend. She would rather spend her entire life alone and practically penniless than to enter into a marriage of convenience, a union without mutual love.

Now that she had reached a conclusion, she lay back and stared up at the view through the glass. With her conclusion had come clarity. Cassiopeia, which had been hidden when she had first searched for her, was now as plain as day. Or night, actually. Peace swept over her as she watched the twinkling stars above, and she knew that even if she could not have all that would make her heart content, she could at least keep her self-respect.

Oh, Grandfather, I hope you are not too terribly disappointed in my decision, Iris mused. She strived to keep his wishes in focus, but the thought of marrying for the sake of a legal document was more than she could bear to do, even for the man who had raised her. *I had no choice, no choice at all.*

His voice filled her head as fully as if he had been sitting beside her. The gruff sound, designed to conceal his soft heart, made her throat tighten.

There are always choices to be had. Do not forget you are a Newgate, and as such you should not settle for less than you want or less than you deserve. Be certain the choices you make are the right ones for you. Follow your heart, Iris. It will never steer you wrong.

She sighed. It was impossible to follow a heart that had a mind of its own, one that refused to listen to reason.

The creak of old hinges commanded her attention. She sat up and looked to the door. A figure approached, cloaked in darkness. She thought to cry out and ask a name, but he moved so swiftly, there was not time to utter a word.

His chuckle, so deep and familiar, sent goose bumps up her arms.

"I thought I might find you here. It seemed a suitable place for you, somewhere you would feel right at home. Ah, yes, surrounded by books and in solitude, with a wondrous view to enjoy. Yes, I was sure this would be where I would find you."

James leaned against the window frame, a nonchalant air making him almost too devilishly handsome in his evening wear. The black jacket and trousers faded into the background, leaving only the starched white shirtfront beneath his face in brilliant contrast. His face was cast in shadow, but she did not need to look upon him with her eyes to see him in her mind.

Two can act detached, Iris thought.

It would serve no purpose to allow James to perceive her feelings toward him. His alliance with Graham—and the delight he had showed earlier over her discomfort at having her acquaintance with the man out in the open—had spoken louder than words could have. He cared nothing for her, and as such he deserved to be cut off entirely.

She sat up on the settee, bringing her feet to the floor and arranging her skirt so that it fell in waves around her velvet slippers. Then she forced a cool tone into her voice and steeled herself for what would most likely be one of the last conversations they would have.

"'A suitable place'? Whatever do you mean? And," she added, "how is it that you feel you know me so well that you can pick and choose, from the endless rooms here at Elliot House, which would be the one most 'suitable' for me to occupy?"

James did not seem put off in the least by her icy questions. If anything, he seemed more pleased than ever. It rankled her that he should take such joy in her discomfort and find no offense in her less-than-friendly stance. Truly, if this was the measure of the man she had declined, hers was a decision she should never have a moment of regret for having made.

She wished she could see his face with her eyes, rather than her mind. It might make connecting her palm with his cheek a simpler task than it would be to do so under cover of darkness. She knew that if he did not ease off the self-satisfied posture, his cheek was going to sting before another star flickered in the sky showing through the glass behind him.

"You are not as obscure as you allow yourself to think, Iris."

James sounded smug and clearly amused. He chuckled again as he came closer still. Now there were only a few feet separating them. Iris gauged the space between her knees and his body; if she stood, she might bump into the man.

Control. She must gain some sense of control over their conversation. Feeling as if she were passenger on a runaway coach gave her the collywobbles.

Taking a deep breath and then slowly exhaling it, she focused her attention back to the starry sky visible through the window behind James' head. The scene soothed her.

"I heard your journey was difficult. I am sorry to hear that but am glad to know that you and your friend, as well as your servants, were not hurt," James said.

"Yes, it is fortunate that no one was injured." The only way James could know about the carriage crash was from Anne. He was in no position to speak with the lady's maids, so Anne was the only one who would have spread the news. Jealousy, an emotion Iris rarely succumbed to, prodded her to say, "It appears you have no need for *The Daily Gazette,* does it? Why, you seem to have a source for current events that far outstrips any journalist they might have in their employ. Fortunate for you, I daresay."

He laughed, the full, hearty sound echoing in the room. The sound of it sent a shiver up Iris' spine and warmth pooling in her center. She liked hearing him so, although the merriment was, once again, at the expense of her pride.

"Oh, but you are something else entirely! And that, I assure you, is meant as a compliment." James paused. He stared down at her for a long moment. "Does it bother you that Anne and I are friends, then? I would think it would not, seeing as how she has made many overtures at befriending you as well."

"Of course it does not bother me! What an absurd notion! And you are right—Anne and I are friendly, although I do not see how that is any of your concern."

He crossed his arms over his chest. The motion made his shoulders look even larger than they were. Now his body blocked her view of the constellation that had become her favorite, but Iris did not care. She was too busy trying to keep herself in check to worry overmuch about Cassiopeia.

"Everything about you is my concern, Iris." He sat beside her on the settee, the movement lightning fast. It was not a large piece of furniture. With James occupying his share, Iris felt nearly squeezed against its arm. His cologne, the same scent that had recently invaded her dreams, swept over her and made it no small feat to keep her mind on his words. "Have you given any thought to my proposal? I said I would not pressure you, but since the deadline is here, it does not seem an unreasonable request to know of your decision."

"The deadline is still"—she did a rapid mental calculation—"nine days from now."

"Nine days—nine hours—nine years! Does it matter how many days there are left? Does your decision hinge solely on the prescribed time limit?"

He raked a hand through his hair. A lone curl fell across his forehead, just begging to be put back into place. Iris ignored it and its pull on her by averting her eyes and concentrating on her hands. They were twisted like tendrils of a grapevine in her lap, her fingers twined so tightly that, had she not been so consumed by other thoughts, they would have pained her.

Prolonging the inevitable was useless. She said softly, "I have already come to a decision."

Silence fell heavily between them.

Finally, James asked, "What is your decision?"

He could not possibly care for her. Playacting, pretending to share feelings he did not have—he *could* not have, she believed—was too silly by far. She would tell the unvarnished truth, and they would put an end to this farce.

"I am going to accept the cottage and stipend offered in my grandfather's will," she said. Sadness brought a catch to her voice, but she refused to let it take hold. She swallowed, determined not to cry at any cost. Later, when she was alone, she would indulge her emotions, but now she would remain strong. She had to keep a stiff upper lip. After all, as Grandfather had reminded her for her whole life, she was a Newgate, and that counted for something. Wiping the tremor from her voice, she went on. "I am flattered by your offer, but I have no choice but to refuse you."

As she spoke, she imagined he would leave the room. She thought he would be relieved that she had not pulled him into a sham of a marriage. She assumed he would sigh, smile, or perhaps even thank her for her levelheaded good sense.

Iris had not bargained on James having a show of temper. He did not lash out, did not shout or carry on. He did not raise a fist in anger, but it was clear by the bite in his voice that he was irritated.

"Why?" One word, spoken so low and with such control. There was no doubt in Iris' mind that she had provoked his temper.

She strove to explain, speaking so quickly that her words fell over one another. "It is for the best. You know it, and I know it—we both know you do not love me, that your offer of betrothal was just a display."

"You sound very sure of yourself." James did not sound as angry as he had before.

Iris took it as a good sign and relaxed somewhat. She spread her hands over her skirt, conscious suddenly that they were cramped from being held so strongly.

"I am," she answered. "Quite sure." She wished she was not, but she was.

"Would you mind explaining yourself to me, then, so I may be as sure as you so clearly are? You say my offer of marriage is a 'display'—of what? And for what purpose?"

James brought his face close to hers. She saw the intensity in his gaze and wished she could just fall into the deep blue eyes and lose herself there. But that was not to be. She had to accept her fate, choose the best of the options at her disposal, and—perhaps the most crucial point of the entire matter—spare as many feelings and futures as she possibly could.

Truth. She had to tell the truth and let the pieces fall wherever they may.

"Please, let's not play games." Iris heaved a huge sigh. "We are both aware of your . . . ah, of your notoriety." She began cautiously, not sure of his reaction, but when James remained silent, she went on. "Now, I am not going to say whether or not I believe any of the gossip or rumors, but I do think that it might be in your best interest to find a suitable wife. Someone who might give your . . . ah, scandalous adventures a slight toning down, if you know what I mean. You might be less newsworthy if you had a dull wife, don't you think? Therein lies the root of your 'display.' "

"And you believe you would be a 'dull' wife?" His voice dripped sarcasm.

Iris swallowed. Of their own accord, her hands had balled themselves tightly in her lap again. "Yes, I do think myself somewhat ordinary. Certainly, by the standards you are familiar with, I must seem horribly dull."

James laughed out loud, the sound so unexpected that Iris gave a little jump. Her skirt left the settee, and a hand went to her chest, bringing more laughter bubbling out of the man beside her.

"You could never be dull, Iris. Believe me, you are so refreshing, I feel like I am out-of-doors when I am near you. In addition, the only thing about you that I have come to expect is that you will surprise me, some way or another, whenever I see you. You, dull? Never!" He slapped a hand on his thigh, the smacking sound making Iris start again. James stopped laughing instantly and peered intently into her eyes. "Why do you jump when I move? Do you believe all that is said about me, then? Do you think the whispered words, spoken behind fans and locked doors, the tales of my nefarious behavior and shocking crimes, hold true? Do you believe that I am what people say I am, Iris? Do you?"

It matters to him what I think, she thought with startling clarity.

"I . . . I do not know what to believe," she answered. It was the truth.

"Fair enough," James said. He sat back, crossed one leg over the other, and stared silently out the window. When she thought the discussion was at an end, he spoke. This time she did not jump. "I can see why you might think that a wife would give my position some credence. I must admit that I, too, thought that very same thing. For a while I considered a wife a necessary accessory. Someone who would, as you say, 'tone down' the scandalous stories surrounding me." James paused. He ran a hand along his trouser leg, stretching his fingers out. She saw they had been curled up, the same ways hers had been, and now he was making what looked like an attempt to relax them. "However, I have lately realized a truth about myself that I did not know before, something that took me by surprise when I did learn it."

"What?" She held her breath.

"I know now that just any woman will not do for me. I do not simply want someone to lend respectability to my character, Iris. I want—" He turned his gaze upon her face. "I want a wife in more than name only. I do not want a marriage of convenience. I want a marriage based on love."

Iris' heart beat so hard, she was sure James must be able to hear it. Had he said what she thought he had?

She stared at him, not having any idea what to say. They both wanted the same thing—that was clear. But that did not mean they were fated to find that common ground together, did it?

"Don't say a word," James said. He reached for her hand, and she let him take it. His skin was warm on hers, and the lazy thumb he swept across the palm of her hand sent tingles to every point in her body. "I cannot expect you to understand me, or how I feel, without providing you with an explanation. Actually, I must explain several things. I have done some checking on your character, and, remember, I was very close with your grandfather, so I know you can be trusted with . . . any and all secrets."

He checked my background?

"It's nice to know I inspire trust—especially since you apparently checked for any skeletons in my closet." The glib retort rolled from her tongue without conscious thought. Iris saw a flicker of amusement in James' eyes, felt the tightening of his fingers on hers, and found she somehow could not begrudge him the investigation of her character.

"You will see that it was necessary. Now, for the explanations. I will not go fully into every detail at this hour, for the details can all be revealed at our leisure, and, while they are an integral part of the puzzle, they are not the entire puzzle, so I shall do my best to keep this simple."

Iris raised an eyebrow in question. They had not gotten to the first explanation, whatever that meant, and already their conversation seemed convoluted and mysterious. Whatever could he be getting at? And would he get to the meat of things before the sun rose?

"Right. Bear with me, please. All will be revealed, eventually. For now, I will say that I am not what the gossips make me out to be. I am not a rogue, a rake, a scoundrel, or the devil himself. I am none of those things. Nor am I a murderer." He stopped, held her hand just a tiny bit tighter, and stared into her eyes. She kept her gaze steady, refusing to waver or blink. Evidently that satisfied him, because he went on. "I know I am supposed to be all those things, and more besides, but I am not. I am held accountable, in scandalized whispers, of course, for the deaths of the missing barons. Notice I said the *missing* barons. I did not say the *dead* barons."

The full effect of his words sank in. *If the barons are not dead, where are they?* Iris wondered. Then she remembered the night of the Vauxhall musicale.

"Lord Holmes was dead. The night you showed me the stars, when you—" Iris caught herself. She had almost reminded him of their clandestine kiss. "When we were walking outside the music hall, a woman found a murdered man. A baron, remember?"

"Certainly, I remember. I remember the music. I remember the stars. I remember our walk. I remember *everything* about that night, Iris." James looked meaningfully at her. Heat flooded her cheeks beneath his gaze. "I remember the baron as well. You are right—he was murdered—but that murder is a separate incident from the list of five missing barons. The ones who have gone missing—Byron, Dashell-Pembroke, Stankman, Oliver, and Pickering—they are the ones I am supposed to have murdered. But they are not dead, merely missing. And they are not actually missing, either. They have been relocated, on the Prince Regent's orders."

The Prince Regent? But that must mean—

Understanding flooded her mind. She was too stunned to speak. Then she managed to gasp, "You work for the Crown?"

James smiled and then nodded. The curl that had lain across his brow all this time fell over his eye. Iris could not stand not being able to see the look in his eyes when he spoke. She needed to see his expression, as well as hear him, as he continued. Without thinking, she reached up and swept the lock of hair back into place. He smiled at her touch—more broadly than she had ever seen him smile. Had she not been so amazed by his words, she might have taken more pleasure in his features, but now all she wanted was to hear more by way of explanation.

She urged him to continue. "Truly? The men are not dead, and you are . . ."

"In His Majesty's service. Undercover, of course. Prinny and I are actually very good friends. Graham, as well, is in the inner circle and is part of the behind-the-scenes machinations that keep this country running like clockwork."

Graham! In her excitement, Iris had forgotten about him. But James must know she had been alone with the man in the park. It was almost too embarrassing to bear! She looked down at her lap, unable to meet his gaze.

"*I* sent Graham to the park that day, Iris."

James' words hit her full force, and she raised her face instantly. The man might get his cheek slapped after all! How could he have tempted her to ruination like that? She had been sad and lonely and had made an error in judgment. Goodness, if anyone found out, she would be completely ruined. And to think of all her subsequent embarrassment! And he had done that intentionally?

He rushed to explain, holding his free hand up between them. "I had to know more of you, how you would act under unusual circumstances. Don't you see? The secrets I must keep—the ones that I will entrust to you—could put the entire country's safety at risk."

"You had to know how I would behave with a charming stranger. . . ."

"I had to know for the sake of the Crown," James answered quietly.

Had the country's security not been an issue, she might have been angered, but, with his explanation so logical and clear, how could she be? She remembered something. "But I did confide in Graham. I told him *my* secret."

Her heart, which had begun to swell, sank to her toes. She tried to pull her hand away from his, but James was stronger. He held on tightly and leaned closer.

"You confided a young woman's worries, true, but nothing of import about anyone else—and not even your own full name!" He paused. "That day in the park I wanted to know if you could behave in any fashion that could hurt Prinny and the whole of England. It was not for me that I tested you. It was for our country. But were I to test you again, were I to throw a flatterer your way now to see how you would comport yourself, it would not be for Prinny. It would not be for national security. If I were to test you again, Iris, it would be for me and me alone. I love you, Iris—with all my heart."

The declaration stole the breath from her body. The world around her dimmed, then swirled. For an instant, she felt light-headed.

James pulled her against his body, holding her close and whispering into her hair. "Not again, Iris. Don't tell me you are trussed up in one of those confounded garments again, the way you were at the Fall Fete. Is your corset too tight? Are you going to swoon again? Iris! Iris, talk to me, please—"

A giggle escaped her lips. She tipped her head back and stared into James' eyes. He loved her! And she . . . goodness, she loved him so much, it made her dizzy to think of it.

She could almost hear Grandfather's words, telling her that she was a Newgate and had only to follow her heart. She could hear the elderly man . . . almost.

Right now, all Iris wanted to hear was James telling her again that he loved her. But first, she had a confession to make.

"No, I am not going to swoon," she said, smiling up at him. His brow cleared, and a look of relief washed over his handsome features. He relaxed, but he did not release her, and she did not pull away from him. "Did you say you love me?"

She had to hear it again.

He nodded. "I did. And I do. Very much, Iris."

"I thought that was what you said." She took a deep breath, trying to commit the glimmer in his eyes to her memory. This moment would be etched on her heart forever, and she did not want to miss one detail. A quick glance through the window at Cassiopeia over James' shoulder was the last bit she needed. "I love you, too. I have for a while now, although I do not think I fully realized it until the night you . . . well, until the night you kissed me. I knew it then, and I know it now. I love you, James."

He furrowed his brow. "But you still refused to marry me. Was it because of my reputation?"

She shook her head. "No, not because of that. I told you that I could not marry a man in name only. I knew how I felt about you, but until just a few moments ago I did not know your feelings for me. It would have been easy, and pleasant, to marry you for the sake of the will and every other little polite excuse I might conjure, but I could not wed a man who did not love me in return."

A slow smile lit James' face. The lock of hair fell over his eye again. Iris reached up and smoothed it back and left her fingers in the thick black silkiness near his brow.

"And now?" he asked. "Will you marry me now, knowing that I love you more than I ever dreamed I could love anyone? Will you consent to be my wife, even though I do come with some unusual circumstances and secrets?"

Iris nodded, knowing there were no circumstances that could keep her from marrying James, no secrets that would ever tear them apart.

"Yes, I will marry you now, James. And I will love you forever."